Susan Bounty

A NOVEL BY

PETER HOLLAND

November 2020

Peter Holland

GW00691758

Brigand
London

Brigand Press,
All contact: info@brigand.london

Cover design
www.scottpearce.co.uk

British Library Cataloguing-in-Publication Data
A catalogue record for this book is
available from the British Library
Printed and Bound in Great Britain by CPI
Group (UK) Ltd, Croydon CR0 4YY

ISBN: 9781912978229

Author's notes and thanks

Susan Bounty is my third novel, following *Barbary Slave* and *1656*. There are links between the three, but in this novel I have moved from my original main subject, slavery, featured in the first two. Whilst researching and writing *1656*, I became increasingly fascinated by the figure of Oliver Cromwell, along with the issues of political, social and religious tolerance, or intolerance, that surfaced in the decade when England was a Puritan republic.

Susan Bounty was real, but little is known about her, which allowed me to create her background, along with adding her lover's character. I enjoyed including other real figures, such as John Milton, a true giant of English Literature, who really was Secretary for Foreign Tongues in Cromwell's government. My interpretation of Cromwell is sympathetic, which will differ to that of others, whether he was 'hero or villain' being one of the great questions of English, British and Irish history. Most of the other characters are fictitious, and I had fun naming and basing some of them on friends I admire.

Finally, for the help and support I have received, my thanks go to David Bryan, Chris Douglas, Allen Peppitt, Philip Tew, and of course, Scott Pearce.

Chapters

September 1652

In her home town of Honiton, Susan Bounty was helping her parents with their display of fabrics at the weekly market. They lived in the town, but her father travelled the county and beyond to buy and sell a variety of materials to shops, markets and individuals. It meant he was sometimes away for several days, even one or two weeks, if he ventured as far as Bristol and once a year to London. Jonathan Bounty missed his small family, consisting of his wife Anne, Susan and her two younger siblings, James aged eleven, and Alice aged thirteen. However, the profit to be made by travelling to buy cloth other merchants could not supply in their corner of Devon provided them with a comfortable living. From time to time merchants would come to Honiton, knowing of Jonathan Bounty, to see if he would be interested in their wares. This was how Susan met William Fogg, a man of thirty years who was skilled in the art of conversation and charm, which he used to good effect in his trade, as well as socially when he was away from home.

Travelling from Bristol with fabrics from across the seas, William Fogg would, like Jonathan Bounty, be away from home for days, sometimes weeks. He had a reliable portfolio of clothiers and fabric tradesmen throughout the south-west and became familiar with his customers and their families. So it was that he had come to know Susan since she was an adolescent girl and then in 1652 as a young woman. Several years earlier he had first noticed the girl changing as she went through puberty, which turned to an unavoidable admiration as her body developed the curves that nature intended for attracting the gaze of men. 'Every time I return to Honiton to do business with Mr Jonathan Bounty, I find myself looking forward to seeing how the fair maid has grown,' he thought to himself as he sat on his cart on the road from Bristol to Exeter. Having stopped at Taunton to pay a visit to a clothier, he should have proceeded south-west on the main road for the last twenty-five miles or so, which was a full day. However, he was drawn southwards on the smaller road towards Ilminster, then turning south-west along the ancient Fosse Way, built by the Romans 1,500 years earlier, to Honiton. He could stay there a night or two, before continuing the last twelve miles to Exeter. Honiton was always worth visiting anyway as it was an excellent manufactury of fine lace. His wife knew his journey would vary in time away depending on trade and he could always return with a nice piece of lace to appease any complaint she might express.

William Fogg had known other women through his time away, usually ladies in taverns on the road, often widows who needed some pennies to supplement their paltry incomes, sometimes women abandoned by feckless husbands who found being a provider too difficult. He stayed away from whorehouses and their dangers of contracting the pox, but he saw no reason not to enjoy the warmth of a mature woman's body, particularly if she was still pleasing to a man's eye. In fact, he had come to look forward to his travels. Treating them kindly, the best ones appreciated the financial assistance he could provide, the result being he knew of six or seven throughout the towns of south-west England who were pleased to see him when he visited on business. It was to his advantage that discretion was essential for such women, as much as it was for him, particularly since the morality laws passed by the Puritan Parliament in 1650, as a woman risked servitude in the Americas if found guilty of whoring.

A man experienced in understanding women, Fogg had time to think as his two horses pulled his cart through the verdant Devon countryside at a slow but steady rate. 'Why am I drawn to Jonathan Bounty's daughter? It cannot end well. I should keep to the older women who are happy to see me for a night once every month or two. They know how to please me and bid me farewell with a smile and a kiss. Even better if they no longer bleed each month, as there is no fear of bastards.' But despite this awareness, Fogg could not stop himself as he diverted from the more direct route to Exeter to visit Honiton in the hope of seeing Susan.

The old Fosse Way road to Honiton climbed a steep hill and Jonathan Bounty's clothier shop was situated in a small road within sight of the Church. Fogg felt a nervous frisson as he turned the corner and saw the girl attending to a customer, a woman dressed in Puritan black but with a lace collar of the highest quality and a fine pair of soft leather shoes, denoting wealth. Susan was helping what appeared to be the woman's young son load drapes onto the back of a horse, which once secure was led away by the sad-looking boy.

'Thank you, Miss Bounty. You are a credit to your parents. Your dear mother is fortunate to have your assistance when your father is away trading his wares. Now, boy! Lead the horse carefully, I do not want these new drapes to fall into the dirt of Honiton High Street. Good day Miss Bounty.' With those words the wealthy Puritan turned and walked past Fogg's cart and onto the High Street. The boy, who Fogg was now uncertain whether he was a son or servant because of the woman's tone, followed guiding the horse with due care.

'Good day, Miss Bounty!' Fogg called before Susan had disappeared into the shop. In her modesty she had kept her head low and had not noticed the man driving the cart. Startled, she looked up and seeing who addressed her she gave a wide smile. 'Hello, Mr Fogg. My apologies, sir, I did not see you there.' Fogg felt a warm feeling at the sight of her smile, as well as embarrassment as he felt an urge stirring in his groin.

'Dear beautiful lady, you have nothing for which to apologise. I feel guilt for not being quicker to assist you in your toil with those heavy drapes.' Now it was Susan's turn to feel an embarrassment at Mr Fogg's compliment, which she knew he would not have expressed in the company of others, but she could not help a feeling of pleasure at his flattery. Her cheeks turned a gentle rouge and she could not suppress a smile. Fogg saw the look on the girl's face and it gave him hope. 'Excuse me, sir.' Showing due modesty, Susan turned and disappeared into her parents' shop to tidy the shelves that had been disturbed by the visit and purchases of the Puritan woman and young boy.

'Good day to you, Mrs Bounty,' Fogg announced with a charming smile on entering the small shop, where thick scrolls of drapes and fabrics filled the shelves that reached the ceiling and covered the tables. Anne Bounty turned holding several pairs of scissors she had used to carefully cut the fabric to the requirements of the recent customer. 'Good day to you, William Fogg, it is always a pleasure to see you here in Honiton.'

The conversation that followed was polite and friendly with Anne explaining to William's disappointment the absence on business of husband Jonathan.

'It is of no importance, Mrs Bounty, I was just passing along this way and decided to stay in a local inn.'

'Sir, we cannot have you stay there when we have a spare bed. You are most welcome to rest at our home, join us for dinner and continue on your journey in the morning.' Anne Bounty liked William Fogg, as did her husband, having got to know him over the last eight years or more.

'Ah, that is most kind of you, Mrs Bounty, but I will feel more comfortable staying at the inn, unless you are in any danger and require protection. In these days of Puritan morality and Justices of the Peace enforcing Parliament's will in all corners of the country, it would not do to provide food for malicious gossip.' William knew that despite not taking the opportunity to observe the young maid and get to know her better, this display of awareness for being seen to being mindful of propriety, would stand him in good stead. However, he would accept the offer of dinner if it still stood.

'I understand, Mr Fogg, and thank you for your propriety. But I insist you come for dinner and you can leave before it gets dark to avoid dangerous gossip.' Anne extended the invitation immediately, to William Fogg's relief. He will be seen to be a gentleman and can enjoy the company of Anne and her daughter. What might follow will wait for another day.

That evening Fogg walked up the hill of Honiton High Street returning to the shop. He did not try to access the main door knowing it was bolted for the night. Instead he entered through a side door in the alley, beyond which he climbed the stairs to the Bounty family living space. With two floors of rooms above the shop, it was a comfortable home and on that first floor he was welcomed into the main room, which served as a place to eat and relax. Anne Bounty, Susan and her two younger siblings all greeted him with smiles, and William was careful to not focus on the maid he found filling his thoughts, but her beauty made this difficult.

Anne had prepared a handsome dish of beef stew, garnished with turnips and carrots. Conversation was polite and led by Anne, her three children showing a respectful deference. However, William took the opportunity to ask of each child's days, which included any studies they might undertake, attendance of the local church and help they were able to provide to their hard-working parents. He asked of Susan's prospects and whether there might be a young suitor, causing the eighteen-year-old to blush, for which he apologised, and was secretly relieved to hear there was presently no such potential threat.

By the end of the meal he was relieved to return to the Ram Inn for the remainder of the evening, where he was able to enjoy a cup of ale and think about Susan before retiring for the night. There would be no warmth from the body of a woman for him that night, but he was pleased with the progress he had made towards something more exciting than the usual encounter he had come to know during his travels around Devon and Cornwall.

October 1652

The Mitre Inn sat almost at the top of Barnet Hill, just yards from the domineering St John The Baptist Church, which faced directly south. Located where the Great North Road, which had started at Smithfield market on the edge of London's city wall, forked to the east before continuing north to York. The other fork proceeded gently to St Albans, the ancient Roman town. The Mitre Inn was almost thirty years old, but the church dated back to the 1250s, built during the reign of Henry III, who faced his own civil war against rebellious barons, led by Simon de Montfort. Two hundred years later the Battle of Barnet was an important battle in another civil war between the houses of Lancaster and York, at which three kings of England fought. However, on this Autumn evening in 1652 a small group of men met, without any intention of rebellion or war, but they did seek change. Former soldiers, who had seen enough of war, they were wise to speak in hushed voices, because what they spoke of could lead to them losing their liberty and lives.

The Mitre was a smoke-filled tavern, the aromatic fog created by some men inhaling through pipes the smouldering tobacco plant imported from the Americas. At a table away from the men smoking and others who stood near the bar, a group of five huddled around a table, speaking quietly. Three of them knew each other from serving in the same regiment over the previous nine years, the other two having come to meet these three for the first time. Identification on entry to the cloudy interior was not easy, but eventually they all spotted the sprig of rosemary each wore discreetly in their hat. A simple piece of the common herb used to flavour food was a secret badge for men who had been called Levellers. Their movement for more rights and equality had been largely quashed, but whilst the organisation had gone, its members remained.

One of the five was a local man, Michael Martin, like the others a soldier and the common acquaintance through whom they came to meet. He was a printer, a very useful trade for the purpose of their causes, and since he had been asked for services by different groups who were dissatisfied with this new England, he decided to speak to them as a collective.

'Good day, gentlemen. Thank you for coming up from London to this southern edge of Hertfordshire,' said Michael Martin, with a tip of his hat. He thought about removing his hat as he was inside the warm, smoke-filled main room of The Mitre Inn, but chose to keep it on, the wide brim offering some security from being easily identified. The other four returned a polite tip of their hats and retained the same protection, further enhanced by keeping their heads leaning slightly forwards, allowing the brim of each hat to hide almost their whole face.

'Thanks to you, sir, for allowing us to meet and share our concerns,' said the man who had arrived last. He had the confident manner of a gentleman, possibly a man of the law, with an accent from the north of England. It was agreed they would not refer to each other by name, instead using a polite sir. The identity of each was shared by Michael Martin through whispers when they first sat down. Those other three men knew of the man who had just spoken, as did every man in the New Model Army, and they were in awe. He was John Lilburne, widely known as Freeborn John, so named for his advocacy of Freeborn Rights, which argued that every man is born with rights. His father and family owned estates in the north, but he was drawn to London, where he could campaign for equal rights for all men. Jeremy Odlin was inspired by being in the presence of a great man who called for suffrage for all men and the right to remain silent in a trial, avoiding the legal trap of incriminating oneself. Lilburne had been put on trial several times, imprisoned, whipped and pilloried for his beliefs and principles. And now he was there in the Mitre Inn, Barnet, meeting men with common ideals.

'Thank you, sir, I am honoured to meet you,' Jeremy Odlin said with another respectful nod. Originally from the hamlet of Crouch End, Jeremy settled in Barnet after marriage to Jane, a woman from Whetstone just one mile to the south of Barnet. The son of a farrier, he rose to the rank of major in Cromwell's cavalry, putting to good effect the skills he learnt riding thousands of horses his father cared for. Jeremy had converted from the established Church of England to the Quakers during his time in the army, after listening to the good, honest men of that simple denomination who believed in simple prayer to the same Christian God, but without the frivolous dressing of bishops and hierarchical structure of a powerful institution. It was only a short step from the purity of simple prayer valued by Quakers to the call for social change of men like Lilburne and the Levellers. More importantly, they were united by being seen as part of the same heretical, seditious movement by Presbyterians, wealthy landowners and MPs in Parliament. The Hertfordshire man was eager to hear what John 'Freeborn' Lilburne had to say. Men born into the privilege of wealthy landowning families, who rose to the rank of lieutenant-colonel, whilst calling for the equality of all men, were not commonplace.

The other two men in the group, David Davies and Gavin Evans, were two Welsh firebrands, who had fought for the Parliamentarian cause believing it would bring change and justice after the Royalists were defeated. They both supported the trial of Charles for treason, and neither was sorry with his sentence, unlike many they had fought alongside. Within the army they had found themselves aligning with men with common beliefs; independent religious groups who wanted greater religious freedom, but also groups calling for a fairer share of the country's wealth. This included every man having the right to vote for MPs as argued by the Levellers, but the two Welshmen had joined the group that became known as Diggers, who went further demanding common ownership of the land by every man, whether he be lord, gentry, or labourer. The Diggers had been quashed, just like the Levellers, but their members also remained and found themselves joining groups of different sects who had merged to gain strength in numbers.

Debates raged throughout the army, between Diggers, Levellers, Quakers and those who were landowners like Cromwell. Whilst Cromwell was sympathetic to some of their ambitions and had considered Lilburne a friend during the war, he found the claims for common ownership of the land beyond reasonable. Like other landowning MPs he saw Diggers as a threat to order and peace. The problem was the overlap of ideas between Levellers, Diggers, Quakers and others. Members of these different groups met and discussed the changes they desired and shared ideas, thereby incriminating themselves in the eyes of their persecutors.

It was through an assumption of guilt by association by those in power that men like Jeremy Odlin, a Quaker, could find himself facing charges of heresy brought by the judicial servants of wealthy landowners. Cromwell was caught in the middle; he had an affinity with men in the army, but he was also now part of the wealthy landowning establishment. For the five men meeting in the Mitre Inn, the man they would follow into battle could not be relied on to protect them from persecution and prosecution under the new heresy and blasphemy laws.

'He's no longer one of us,' David Davies said, 'he was a landowner before the war, but he was a man of the people, and we trusted him.'

'Aye, now he owns palaces,' Gavin Evans added.

'How so?' Jeremy asked.

'Did you not hear, friend?' Gavin replied, 'Parliament gave him Hampton Court, as a family residence, a reward for defeating the Scots at Worcester last year.'

David nodded in agreement with his countryman from the other side of the Black Mountains. 'That be true, we were both there, Gavin. Parliament did not give us a hut or an acre!' With that he took a deep draft of the fine Hertfordshire ale that made the journey to High Barnet worthwhile.

Michael Martin was of Irish ancestry, his paternal grandparents having been church reformers following Luther's

teachings, who came across the sea during the reign of
Gloriana. But now he, like so many, sought further reform,
both religious and social. Michael had entered the Mitre Inn
stooping, as he did through most doors due to his height. Inside
he had to lean slightly forward lest his head scraped the ceiling,
and only once seated could the man, who measured almost two
yards in height, straighten his back. 'Friends, we have come
here from different groups, he said, 'but we have common
ambitions.'

'Indeed, Michael. We all want a more equal England,
and we are stronger together,' John Lilburne said, drawing
nods and approving grunts from the other four.

'Aye, but how do we go about achieving our common
aims, short of another war?' David Davies asked. 'Aye, that's
the problem,' his countryman, Gavin Evans echoed. The heads
and eyes of four men turned to John Lilburne, the articulate
man from the north, waiting for an answer as he took a deep
breath.

'Petitions.' One word was his answer.

'Petitions? Is that the best you can offer?' David asked.
Jeremy raised his eyebrows, glancing at Michael sitting across
the table. Both of the Barnet men were keen to hear more and
be persuaded that co-operation between different groups,
whether they be Quaker, Leveller or Digger, could bring about
a change for the better.

'Do not underestimate the power of popular protest
through signatures, friends,' Lilburne continued. 'It is a
clear statement to government of the will of the people, and
Parliament will be well-aware of the danger of ignoring that
after these last ten years.' Lilburne was a skilled orator and had
taken control, and the others again nodded as they leaned in
over the table to hear more. 'We should agree some demands
common to all our causes, upon which a document can be
drafted. Then we can work within our groups to gain support
and most importantly, signatures. Parliament will find it hard
to ignore a document signed by tens of thousands, particularly

if many of them are soldiers, or former soldiers.' He paused, looking at each of the four men, all recently serving men in the New Model Army.

'Yes, sir. You might be onto something there,' Michael said, 'I would like to see them ignore that. 50,000 signatures would make them sit up and listen.'

'What if a man supporting our cause does not know how to write, sir?' Gavin asked, 'some soldiers did not know of schooling, particularly if they were raised on remote farms in Wales, miles from the nearest village or town.'

'Aye, I am embarrassed to confess I've never held a quill, sir.' David spoke in support of his friend. 'It was two hours to our closest village, which we managed most Sundays to worship the Lord, weather permitting. Otherwise we only got close to a school on market day.' He looked down at the table in shame. Lilburne looked at the Welshman, humbled by his honesty and felt some admiration that a man with no education could become a Sergeant in the army and had found a cause to help his fellow man.

'Do not fear, friend,' Lilburne replied. 'Each man can make his own mark and his name can be written next to it. Your name will be there with thousands who enjoyed the privilege of an education, David.' With that Lilburne reached across the table to grasp David Davies' hand, who looked up at the great man, 'Thank you, sir.'

What followed was a conversation at which each man was heard, and numerous examples of injustice were shared. Lilburne's task was to bring them together, united in demanding three, four, or five guarantees. Finally, after several pints of ale, more than an hour had passed and he was able to bring the meeting to a close.

'So, friends, we are in agreement. A Grand Petition shall be drafted calling for Parliament to provide all men with the following: Firstly, every man in England and Wales should be allowed to vote for an MP as a representative for his parish and other parishes of his area. Secondly, no man should be forced to speak at his own trial, for fear of incriminating himself. Thirdly, all men and their families should be free from persecution to worship our Christian God as their consciences decree.' Lilburne glanced around the main room of the Mitre Inn as he made these statements, well aware that government spies were everywhere. In hushed voices only the five men could hear, each of the other four replied, 'Aye.'

'Thank you, friends. Our brother, Michael, will produce copies of the petition, which we will share with like-minded men, for the purpose of collecting names and signatures. Let us shake hands, and agree to meet in ninety days, after which I will take our Grand Petition to Westminster.' As he finished, Lilburne reached across the table to shake the hand of the other four, who repeated the same gesture.

Outside the sun was getting lower and three members of the group had to make haste to get back to London before darkness enveloped the great city. All three had horses ready to ride the twelve miles south downhill, leaving Jeremy and Michael to walk together for ten minutes until their paths home separated.

'Michael, we found consensus with these men, but their ambitions are greater than ours, we being merely Quakers seeking freedom to worship God as we wish without persecution,' Jeremy said quietly, furtively glancing over his shoulder to see if anyone might be within earshot. 'But you know it is a great risk we take, you greater than me, if we are seen to align ourselves with the changes they demand of Parliament.'

'Aye, I know,' Michael replied, 'but we cannot achieve our ends alone, hoping the men in power look kindly upon us. Those who follow the teachings of Calvin, like the Presbyterians, are as intolerant of reform as were the Catholics at the time of Luther's protests. They all see us as heretics, Jeremy.' Michael knew of the danger to which his friend referred, which left him uncertain about their future, but his mind was set. 'An alignment between our different groups, with a petition signed by tens of thousands, offers us strength in numbers, my friend.' Michael chose to not dwell on the risk, focusing instead on what might be achieved.

'Michael, we must be clear in our minds. If we are found to be the organisers of such a petition by powerful men who oppose us, our fates could be very dark,' Jeremy said as they reached the divide in their paths, taking each to his home.

'I know, Jeremy. Sleep well, friend.'

November 1652

'I had rather that Mahometanism were permitted amongst us, than one of God's children should be persecuted!' Oliver Cromwell bellowed across the floor of the House of Commons. Just earlier that year in February he had persuaded Parliament to pardon all acts of treason committed before Worcester. How could Parliament argue with the man who six months earlier had saved England from a successful invasion by the Scots and remaining Royalists? Since then MPs had undermined his appeals for clemency, some whispering amongst themselves that their saviour sought to pardon delinquents, criminals and traitors to swell his ranks of supporters. But he was tired of the persecution of dissenters by men of power, often by Presbyterians who continued to display intolerance of fellow Christians. 'Damn these Calvinists,' he thought to himself as he made his way to the terrace overlooking the Thames, where he had an appointment with a young officer, whose counsel he valued more highly than those infernal MPs. There at the end of the terrace stood the young officer, and Cromwell's mood lifted slightly.

'Good day, Major Flain. Thank you for coming at such short notice,' Cromwell said, admiring the army man in the prime of his life. He was not the tallest officer, but he was strong and handsome, with a complexion that was not pale, suggesting a life lived outside. 'How goes it in the army? I miss the men and long to be with them, rather than here in this place,' he added, glancing back at the Palace of Westminster.

'The army is in turmoil, sir,' Major Flain said with some nervousness, not knowing what the response would be. Oliver Cromwell looked at him with a glare, and for a moment Flain thought he had over-stepped the mark, daring to express a view on so serious a matter. But he was reassured by the response of the supreme leader of the army. Cromwell's glare was an expression of his horror that the institution he had modernised and led with Fairfax was in danger of falling into chaos.

'Sadly, this is not news to me, Major. I am increasingly hearing whispers of discontent amongst our comrades, men with whom we have become brothers through these last ten years of war here in England, Ireland and Scotland. Please God, I hope the defeat of the Scots and the last of the Royalists at Worcester barely a year ago will be the end of battles being fought on these islands for some time,' Cromwell said with a solemn voice.

Major Steven Flain was a professional soldier, devoted to the man who was seen by thousands in the army as a saviour for their country and the ordinary man. The major had come from modest stock, just a small farming family in Hertfordshire near the village of Welwyn. He joined the Parliamentarian cause, tired of the arrogance of King Charles and his notion of the Divine Right of Kings to rule as they wished, Parliament being no more than a conduit to raise revenue through taxation. The New Model Army, created by Cromwell and his superior officer General Fairfax, provided men like Steven Flain with equality and opportunity they had never previously known. Before the Civil War it would have been unheard of for men like him to rise to senior ranks. Indeed, Cromwell himself was of modest means before rising to Colonel and now General.

'Please God, let it be so, sir,' the young major echoed.

'It is only two years since the mutiny of almost half the army marched on London, resulting in imprisonment and execution of so many of our brothers. Were we wrong to oppose them, Major?' Cromwell was asking the young officer a question he had asked himself many times, along with so many others in the army.

'Sir, you did what you thought was right at the time. Anarchy and chaos could have followed, and you were upholding the rule of law,' Flain replied with honesty, but like his leader wondered if they should have joined the revolt and completely removed the self-serving Parliament the mutiny sought to overthrow.

'The law? Aye, we know about the law, Major. Laws are passed by Parliament for the benefit of the people, but how they are used by men in power is the problem.'

'Indeed, sir. Our men have been impoverished with fines for transgressing the new morality laws, as well as persecuted for seeking a freedom of conscience to worship our Christian God as they choose,' Flain said, 'and Parliament seems to have an army of lawyers and judges to interpret the new laws in their favour.'

'I've discussed this many times with my trusted friend, Edmund Ludlow, Major Flain. He is a rare beast, a man of the law and a damn fine soldier, and he agreed with me,' Cromwell said.

'Yes, sir. May I enquire what it was you agreed upon, sir?'

'My apologies, Major. My thoughts are ahead of my words. Even two years ago, Ludlow agreed with me when I said to him "the lawyers cry out we mean to destroy property, whereas the law as it is now constituted serves only to maintain the lawyers, and to encourage the rich to oppress the poor!" We've since seen this increase as Parliament and judges prosecute our men for contravening these new laws.'

'Yes, sir. I have seen many men who want the equality and freedom they were promised by Parliament. In the army they met and discussed with like-minded men, and joined the new non-conformist groups. Quakers, Levellers and Diggers are seen as a threat to not just the established churches, but also to rich land-owners, who use the blasphemy and heresy laws to prosecute them.'

Steven Flain summed it up perfectly, confirming Cromwell's fears. He liked the young major.

'Aye, you're right, Major. The question is, what shall we do?'

'Sir, if I spoke my mind and men of power heard my

words, I fear my head might be on a pike decorating London Bridge,' Steven said with half a smile, endeavouring to add some levity to the conversation. Publicly, Cromwell was known as a serious man, not given to humour. Why would he be, having spent a decade fighting wars and finding himself at the forefront of a revolution. However, in private, particularly when in the company of soldiers away from the battlefield, he was given to laughter and enjoying himself.

'Well, we can't have that happening, can we Major? You're far too handsome for that fate at so young an age, and besides there are too many maids bemoaning the loss of English beaus falling in battle. By my word, methinks there could be a petition of thousands of fair signatures being compiled as we speak!' Cromwell did not disappoint Steven Flain with his response and shared a wry smile. 'That being said, I do rely on you and several other officers to keep me aware of the mood of our men, Major Flain. And rest assured, your thoughts are safe with me, as I place great value on honesty and loyalty.'

'Yes, sir,' Steven Flain replied with a sense of privilege and considerable relief.

'Come inside and tell me more about the men, Major,' Cromwell said, and they walked in through a guarded door, where the sentries nodded to the supreme leader, who returned the courtesy and more. 'Good afternoon, Sergeant. Would you and your men care for a warmed ale? It is getting wintry out here.'

'Thank you, sir,' the sergeant said, 'but I think we will be fine, sir.'

'Nonsense, Sergeant, I cannot have my best men catching an ague. I will send an aide out with something to warm the four of you.'

'That is most kind, sir,' the sergeant replied, followed by the other three soldiers all joining him with, 'Thank you, sir.'

They went into the great building, where Cromwell was

able to call one of his aides to supply the sentries at the door with some warm ale and biscuit. Steven observed the exchange and it was not the first time he had witnessed Cromwell's compassion for his men of all ranks. He followed Cromwell into an office, where they were able to speak further for thirty minutes or so, and Steven too was provided with a warmed weak ale.

A while later Major Flain walked out of the offices of state in Westminster Palace into the cold November late afternoon sunshine, which would soon be darkness as the sun began to disappear in the west. Leaving by the same side door through which they had entered, the same four soldiers were there and, on seeing Steven, stood to attention.

'Thank you for the warm ale, sir,' the sergeant said, 'it was most welcome.'

'Thank you, Sergeant, but it was our leader, not I, who thought that you should have some much deserved warm refreshment,' Steven replied, and gave the sentries a courteous nod as he proceeded across the terrace.

His thoughts were of Cromwell, the soldiers and the turmoil within the army. 'Perhaps, there is hope for my Quaker friends,' he thought, 'though I am not sure if even Cromwell can save those former Levellers and Diggers.' With that he headed south to the river to employ the service of a wherryman to get him to Southwark where he was lodging, thereby avoiding the stench of the streets.

Cromwell returned to his study, from where he could see the Abbey and beyond it the river. It was a view he enjoyed when he wanted some solitude for the purpose of thinking. Parliament and powerful men using the new laws to persecute army officers joining non-conformist groups agitating for change. Problems and what to do filled his thoughts as he looked down towards the Thames.

That evening he felt a nausea come across him and realised he was about to have one of his 'episodes,' as Elizabeth referred to them. 'Damn it, damn this malady,' he thought, aware of what was likely to follow. He knew he would be no company for his family, and whilst physicians assured him his condition was not a danger to others, he could not bear the thought of passing it to his family. Therefore, he had an aide take a message by wherry upriver to Hampton Court to tell his wife he would stay in his private quarters for the next couple of nights. 'No need to scare Elizabeth unduly,' he thought, and could not lie to her, so gave no reason.

These attacks seemed to occur on a regular basis since the campaigns in Ireland. 'That country of dampness and bogs did not agree with me, I wish I had never crossed the Irish Sea,' he thought as he tried to eat some mutton stew and bread, but his appetite was failing and he left most of it uneaten, despite the advice by his physicians to eat and drink. He dismissed his aide for the evening, partly because there was nothing that could be done to help him, but also because he was embarrassed to be seen in a state of discomfort and helplessness. Soon enough the episode quickly developed, his nausea joined by a mild sweat which progressed to a fever that soaked his linen shirt, at the same time leaving him feeling cold as chills swept through his body. There was nothing to do but take to his bed, with a jug of water, and wait for it to pass. The bed sheets would be wet and in need of changing in the morning, but that would wait and all he wanted now was to sleep.

'Elizabeth, my dear wife these last thirty-two years,' he thought and turned clutching the outer blanket close, as a wave of coldness wracked his body despite the sweat. 'You have been with me since we had the Scottish King on the throne, with me through the struggle with his fool of a son, the war, and now life in London. Bless you, my love, and bless the nine children you brought into the world.' His thoughts moved to their children, of whom six were alive. 'Our first two sons, Robert and Oliver, died aged eighteen and twenty-two as they were developing into fine men, and dear James a mere infant in his first year. But we still have six, Elizabeth, and I could not bear to see our two youngest daughters, Mary and Frances, who are with you now, suffer this curse.'

Despite the reassurance of physicians, he was uncertain whether he could pass this illness to others. He thought of the examinations he had received by learned men of medicine, and the horror he felt when Dr Wilkins apologised for asking if he had carnal contact with other women, the question asked to eliminate the cause being the pox. Cromwell excused the good doctor, realising it was necessary for the purpose of diagnosis, even allowing an examination of his genitals and naked body for other signs of the dreaded disease that afflicted men and women of loose morality. Dr Wilkins was pleased and relieved to dismiss the malady as being due to the pox.

He kept turning under the blankets in a state of discomfort, staring at the fire that continued to burn on the other side of the room, until sleep finally overcame him.

'Oliver! Fifty-seven former soldiers have been hanged and their corpses now decorate the Tower and London Bridge' Edmund Ludlow said, 'and now there is mutiny in the army!'

'What? How can this be? Who signed their death warrants?'

'You did, Oliver, when you agreed to those laws two years ago,' Ludlow replied.

'Dear God, this cannot be!' Cromwell cried out, 'those laws are not mine, they were passed by Parliament when I was serving the Commonwealth in Ireland and Scotland!'

'Aye, that may be so, Oliver, but after Worcester you are now seen as the most powerful man in England. The people and the army see you living in Hampton Court, a king's palace, with all the finery of a monarch. Some say these laws are to serve you and the other rich and powerful men in Parliament,' Ludlow said, leaning over him.

'I did not ask for the palace, Parliament gave it to me as thanks for Worcester. They are not my laws!' he exclaimed, and as he did so he woke up.

The blankets had been kicked off and lay on the floor

by the bed, and the fire had burnt down, but thankfully he felt some warmth from its heat, and the chill inside his body dissipated. For a moment he lay still, trying to remember more of the dream, with some success, but not all of it. 'Soldiers hanged, mutiny in the army, my fault' he muttered to himself. Then he realised the sheet he was laying on was damp from his sweat, so he rose from his bed, pulled them off and discarded them on the floor. Reaching to the shelf above the bed, he took two clean sheets and laid them down in the light from a solitary candle, collected the two blankets from the floor and got back into his bed.

Perturbed by the dream but relieved the fever had lifted, he laid there whilst looking at the fading embers and trying to make sense of the dream. Finally, he said, 'Thank you, God,' and closed his eyes.

December 1652

Three weeks before Christmas was a good time for William Fogg to visit a few Devon towns, as many clothiers might have orders to fulfil. December in Devon rarely felt the cold that enveloped much of the country, settling snow being quite rare, but if it did fall it would quickly turn to slush, making roads difficult. So, there was a risk between venturing out for a few days in unfavourable conditions, to be balanced against the opportunity to sell cloth. After giving it some thought and procrastinating for a few days he decided to go, and Elizabeth Fogg bid her husband a safe journey. She waved him off from their house and shop in Bristol on a cold but sunny, dry day. In view of the uncertain weather, they agreed he would visit only a few towns on a trip that should last only three to four days.

William's main destination was the city of Exeter, but he would stop at Honiton ten miles to the east, then after Exeter head north to the market town of Taunton in Somerset. From there he could get home to Bristol in a day, weather and road permitting. He used two horses to pull his cart, which was not filled with a heavy load, so progress should be good, and he enjoyed his time away from home, even at this time of the year. If a storm should appear, he would make for the nearest village or town providing shelter, of which there were many in this part of the south-west. Holding the reins as his horses trotted at a comfortable pace, he liked to think about where he might stop, and the possibility of some female company. 'Betsy Carter in Yeovil would be pleased to see me,' he thought to himself, as he left Bristol heading south on the road towards Shepton Mallet. 'She has been left with three children by her useless husband, who appears to have run off to the Americas.' His thoughts continued, 'Despite the hardship of life, she is still a woman with a pleasing shape, fine dark brown hair and a nice smile.' As he thought about Betsy the attraction of stopping in Yeovil grew, along with an urge in his loins, but he knew if he tarried there, he would find it difficult to stop for a night in Honiton. In Honiton he would not enjoy the benefits that drew him to Yeovil, but he found the prospect of seeing young Susan Bounty irresistible. Therefore, he avoided turning off the road and stopping at Yeovil, instead proceeding to Ilminster, hoping the weather would stay fair, allowing him to then continue to Honiton.

As the two horses pulled the cart along the ancient Fosse Way leaving Ilminster, William looked up at the sky to see dark clouds coming from the west. Everyone in the south-west counties of England understood the influence of the great ocean that stretched thousands of miles to the New World, and how it could throw a storm across the land in just an hour.

'Oh no,' William said to himself, and shook the reins encouraging the horses to a more energetic trot.

It was only eighteen miles between Ilminster and Honiton, which at a good trot might take two hours, but if the rain was heavy the road would quickly turn to mud and the journey would become longer, and much wetter.

'Come on, Jessie, get on!' and he gave the horses a firm tap on their hind quarters with his long stick.

By halfway the rain had started to fall, but the road remained firm, so the two horses were encouraged to lengthen their stride, splashing through the puddles that formed across the road. William pulled his hood over his head and concentrated on keeping the horses straight and the cart stable, which despite the worsening conditions took his mind off the rain and cold wind.

Thankfully, an hour after the rain had started to fall, William's two horses reached the bottom of the hill leading up to Honiton, and he was able to let them relax to a gentle trot.

'Easy now, Jessie. You too Mabel,' and the two mares slowed as they climbed the hill towards the church, which had come into sight. Only a couple of weeks until the winter solstice, the sun was getting low, even though it was still the afternoon, so William was relieved to turn off Honiton High

Street onto Carders Lane, the small road where Jonathan Bounty and his family lived above their shop.

'Goodness gracious me, it's Mr Fogg,' Anne said on seeing him enter their shop, soaking wet. 'William, you will catch an ague that will be the death of you. Come in and sit down, please. Jonathan! It's Mr Fogg,' she called towards the rooms at the back of the shop.

'Good day, Mrs Bounty. I apologise for my condition but wanted to call on you before Christmas. However, I misjudged the weather,' William replied with a smile, rainwater dripping from his hair and clothes, just as Jonathan appeared from the back room, where he had been tidying rolls of cloth.

'Dear God, look at you William. You are wet through! Anne, kindly take William upstairs and tell Susan to make sure the fire is stoked,' Jonathan said, and looked outside to see Jessie, Mabel and the cart. 'William, I will take your horses round the back to our stable and bring your wares in for safe keeping,' Jonathan added.

'Jonathan, that is most kind, I could not possibly impose on you,' William replied.

'Nonsense! I insist. You could wander the streets of Honiton looking for a room that is not available, and with the sun setting it is too late to get to Exeter. Anne, would you...'

'Of course, my love,' his wife replied, turning to William, 'Please, Mr Fogg, come this way.'

Upstairs in the main room, a high-backed wooden bench and two comfortable chairs lined the hearth of the open fire, which was burning slowly.

'Sit here, Mr Fogg,' Anne said, gesturing to one of the large chairs. 'Susan, Susan!' she called, and her daughter emerged from one of the rooms. 'Susan, please make Mr Fogg comfortable and tend to the fire. Let me have your coat, and boots, we can get them dry for you overnight.'

'Ah, thank you, Mrs Bounty, but please call me William,' he replied, and settled into the large chair, taking off his boots.

'Well, then I will, but only if you call us by the Christian names with which we were baptised,' Anne said. After some fussing over his coat and boots, Anne left him to be taken care of by her daughter as she went back downstairs to assist her husband, adding as she left, 'I will be back shortly.'

For a moment there was an awkward quiet as neither Susan nor William were unsure of what to say, before William broke the silence.

'Your parents are very kind, Susan. I am most grateful,' he said, looking at the young woman as she bent forwards to tend the fire.

He looked at the shape of her body, which was within touching distance, and he felt embarrassed that he could feel such an attraction so quickly. 'Dear God, she is beautiful,' he thought to himself, and as he admired the curves of her breasts, the urges he felt in his loins made him wonder if he should have stopped in Yeovil to enjoy the company of Betsy. Instead he was here in Jonathan Bounty's living room, entranced by the innocence and beauty of an eighteen year-old girl he knew it would be folly to pursue.

'Yes, sir,' Susan replied, modestly focusing on the fire, which needed more wood, avoiding looking directly at William.

'Please, Susan, call me William, as I requested your mother,' he said leaning forward to assist her by lifting some wood to the side of the hearth, close to his chair. Just as he did so, Susan was moving to the same pile of wooden logs, and not seeing him she bumped into him and stumbled towards the open fire. William instinctively jumped up to catch hold of her and stop her from falling forward.

'Take care, Susan,' he said as he held her safe in his arms for just a moment. For a few seconds their bodies were pressed together, and he could smell the scent of rose oil. Then he released her once she was stood upright and safe.

'Oh, sir, I am sorry, I did not see you,' she said, as if

she was at fault.

'Dear lady, you did no wrong, so have nothing to apologise for. Please, call me William.' He had released his hold on her, but their bodies were still close, and realising she was embarrassed and vulnerable he felt a surge of excitement.

After a few seconds of them standing close, William sat down on the chair, allowing Susan to complete her duty tending to the fire, which within minutes was roaring and throwing out a wave of heat.

Susan had not said anything else, feeling slightly uncomfortable after finding herself in the arms of a man. She was grateful he had saved her from getting burnt, but she also felt a strong frisson through her body as he held her. She was innocent in the ways of the world and of relationships with men, but she knew the feeling was sexual, something she had never experienced before. Slightly confused, she thought it best to complete her work and retire to her room.

'Thank you, Susan. I am sure you have saved me from an ague,' he said, attempting to engage her in conversation.

'Yes, sir, I mean William, and thank you for saving me from falling into the fire,' she replied, and looked up with a modest smile.

William felt emboldened by this and took a chance that he knew could prove to be a mistake. He stood up, moved two steps to Susan, gently took her hand and lifted it to his lips, kissing it lightly. Susan was shocked but did not resist, feeling a further rush of excitement through her body.

'Thank you, Susan,' was all he said sincerely and looked into her eyes.

She stood frozen for a second or two, her head was spinning as a result of what had happened in the previous two minutes. Blood rushed to her cheeks and all she could say was, 'Thank you, William,' before turning and seeking the sanctuary of her room, where she could compose herself and try to comprehend what had happened.

As the door to Susan's room closed behind her,

William could hear footsteps on the stairs, and seconds later Anne Bounty entered the main living room.

'Good, I can see Susan has got the fire going for you, William, but where is she? I hope she offered you something to drink?' Anne said, before calling, 'Susan!'

'Please, Anne, your daughter has been kind and hospitable. I think she just returned to her room to fetch something,' and as William spoke Susan reappeared from her room.

'Susan, bring some cups and we should warm Mr Fogg with some mulled cider.'

'Yes, mother,' and Susan carried out her mother's instructions with quiet modesty.

'William, Jonathan has said he insists on you staying the night. We have a sleeping space at the back of the shop, which is clean, warm and dry. Perhaps not as grand as you might be accustomed to, but better than wandering the streets, or trying to get to Exeter in the dark. I have pork stew for supper. Jonathan is just securing your horses for the night and putting your wares safely away. Then he will join us.'

William was delighted but took care to show a humble appreciation.

'Anne, you are really too kind. I do not want to impose...'

'Nonsense!' Anne interrupted, 'we are pleased to have you visit and stay,' she said.

'Thank you, Anne. I must admit to feeling much better inside your house than I was thirty minutes ago on the road into Honiton,' William said with a smile, and as he did he could see a smile appear on the face of Susan as she stood just to the left and slightly behind her mother.

Supper proceeded in a warm and friendly manner, with Jonathan at one end of the table and Anne at the other. To the delight of both Susan and William, they were seated facing each other at Jonathan's end, with the two younger children facing each other at Anne's end. Conversation was led by

Jonathan, which centred on the cloth industry. He welcomed the opportunity to ask William about the health of other cloth merchants and sellers throughout the south-west region, which William was happy to answer as best as he could, gaining favour with the head of the family. Jonathan then went on to talk about the demise of the cloth industry over the previous 100 years, with increased competition from abroad. Throughout the meal William was careful to pay attention to Jonathan, stealing only glances at his host's daughter facing him across the table, and she too was careful to be a model of modest virtue, keeping her gaze towards her plate, apart from looking up at her father, and occasionally across at William. However, like William she found herself wanting to look directly at him and smile. Anne Bounty's pork stew was excellent, and it was washed down with a fine warmed cider. By the time they had finished eating and drinking, and Jonathan was tired of talking, an hour had passed, and William was invited to join Jonathan in the large chairs by the fire, while Susan and her siblings helped their mother clear up.

'Sit here, William. Tell me about your family and life in Bristol,' Jonathan said, as they settled down having re-filled their cups with cider. William listened and conversed politely with his host, but all the time his thoughts were of Susan and he observed her moving about the room, performing her duties in tidying the house at the end of the day. Eventually the candles were burnt low and it was time for everyone to retire for the night, so goodnights were said. To William's surprise, Jonathan told his daughter to take their guest downstairs to show him the small space at the back of the shop, where his bed had been prepared behind a curtain.

The house was in darkness and shadows provided by candlelight, so once the door to the living room was closed and they descended the stairs, William and Susan were out of sight and sound from the rest of the family upstairs. He knew he must not scare the girl, but it was an opportunity he could not waste. Susan led him through the shop to the space where his bed had been made, and whilst neither had spoken since leaving the main room upstairs, they both felt a nervous anticipation.

'Here you are, sir, I mean William,' she said turning to face him, 'I hope you are comfortable and sleep well,' and she looked down modestly.

'Susan, may I speak very briefly, as I know you must return to your parents.'

'Yes, William, of course.'

'I have been greatly affected by being with you so closely today, and the emotions that have been revealed to me cannot be denied.'

'I know, William. I must confess I too was affected, and I am both confused and a little scared by what it means.'

'Dear girl, do not be afraid. We must stop and go to our beds, but please know my thoughts will be of you tonight when I close my eyes.'

Susan was unsure of what she should say. 'Thank you, William, and I will think of you. But now I must go.'

William knew he had one last gesture. 'Let us write each other a letter, which we can exchange when we meet next,' he said and with his left hand that was not carrying a candle he held her free hand in his, before raising her hand to his lips and kissing it gently. Susan felt an excitement that was previously unknown to her and blushed, her cheeks turning red. 'Would you like that?' he asked quietly, his face so close to hers they could have kissed the other's lips.

'Yes, William, I would like that very much,' Susan said, her head dizzy with emotion.

Minutes later they were both in their beds. William knew what he wanted, whereas Susan did not and wondered what was happening to her.

'William, wait!' Anne Bounty called from inside the shop. He was just about to give Jessie and Mabel a shake of the reins to signal time to leave. Jonathan and their three children were there to wave William on his way, as Anne emerged from indoors with a linen cloth package. 'Here, have this for the journey,' she said handing it to him. 'It's just some fresh bread and cheese, William. I don't want you to go hungry.'

'Ah, thank you, Anne. You have been more than kind. God bless you, and all your family,' William replied with a smile.

'Be sure to return soon, William,' Jonathan said, 'I want to hear more of the state of the cloth trade in other towns.'

'I certainly will, Jonathan, but now I must sadly make my way to Exeter. I hope to be back in a month or two,' William said and caught Susan's eye as he spoke. She was listening intently and smiled when his eyes met hers.

'Good man, William, and safe journey,' Jonathan said and gave Jessie a slap on her hind quarters to encourage her into action.

'Good-bye for now, and see you all soon,' William said turning, waving with one hand as he held the reins in the other. Jessie and Mabel pulled the cart onto Honiton High Street and slowly down the hill, following the road south-west to Exeter.

January 1653

Sir Charles Hadleigh's private quarters inside the Palace of Westminster were warm from the freshly stoked fire, and he closed the door to not only keep the heat in the room but also to avoid any persons passing from hearing their conversation. He was joined by his friends and fellow MPs, Jonathan Marlow and James Banstead, as well as two others he was meeting for the first time, who shared the same concerns.

'Thank you for coming, gentlemen. We are meeting here because we are all concerned over the demands that continue to be made by agitators and dissenters, which are a threat to the natural order we all depend upon,' Sir Charles said.

'Sir Charles, these men are Simon Riches, whose family have owned land in Suffolk since 1415, reward from the fifth Henry for their part at Agincourt, and Paul Gooding from Northamptonshire, whose family owns more than 700 acres,' Jonathan Marlow said.

'Please, Paul, Simon, have these seats,' Sir Charles said, gesturing to the two large chairs closest to the fire.

'Thank you, Sir Charles,' Simon replied as he and Paul settled into the leather furnishings.

'Here, Jonathan,' Sir Charles said, passing two table chairs to his friends, before moving a third for himself. Before he joined them sat down, Sir Charles poured five generous glasses of port from a large decanter sat in the middle of the table from which he had moved the three chairs. The glasses were carefully passed amongst his guests, and they were then ready to commence the meeting.

'Gentlemen, your good health,' he said raising his glass, adding with a smile, 'I have two more bottles in the cupboard.'

'Good health!' the others replied simultaneously.

Paul Gooding and Simon Riches had made the journey

from their homes to London specifically to speak to their MPs and meet others who might listen to their concerns. The wealth of both men and their families was based on the land, which was either rented to other farming families, or occupied by farm labourers who worked the land for the owners in return for a cottage and small patch they could ostensibly call 'theirs,' without legal ownership. Such labourers were the descendants of peasants, who for hundreds of years were at the bottom of the feudal pile.

There had been peasants' revolts and uprisings before, but now the ranks of dissatisfied labourers were swelled by former soldiers, as well as more learned men calling for constitutional change. When the world was turned upside down with Charles' beheading it seemed to give dissenters more courage, and men like Gooding and Riches were getting worried.

'Sir Charles, Paul has personal experience of the consequences of the sedition that is being spouted by the likes of Lilburne,' James Banstead said.

'Please tell me, Paul,' the host replied, looking over to the landowner from Northamptonshire.

'Yes, Sir Charles. We have had a colony of them settle on land we own just outside Towcester, living in some old cottages left empty by the enclosures of the last Henry. The land had been left fallow for some years, and they seem to think that allows them to claim it as belonging to the people,' Paul explained

'Dear God!' Sir Charles exclaimed.

'We've had a similar experience on some land of ours near Sudbury,' Simon Riches added, 'we think they are former Diggers, re-emerging as Levellers.'

'I see,' Sir Charles said, looking at Simon in the comfortable leather chair the other side of the fire. 'It is getting worse.'

'Indeed,' Jonathan Marlow said, 'if more spring up, and they join together under a cause or banner, we could have a major uprising on our hands.'

'Have you tried using force? Surely a small militia could clear them off the land?' Sir Charles asked.

'They are men, women and children, Sir Charles, but many of the men are former soldiers, and brazenly speak of the support they have from within the army. They have a few muskets, but they all know how to wield a pike and a sword!' Jonathan replied and the two landowners nodded in agreement.

'If successful in clearing them off the land, where do they go?' Paul said, 'just to the next piece of land that is not occupied. So, we are simply moving the problem from one piece of fallow land to the next.'

'Also, if we are seen to take forceful measures against people who now pose as Quakers, how will that be received by those in the army who sympathise with their cause?' Simon asked.

'What is to be done then?' James Banstead asked. and for a few moments there was quiet as the five men of wealth and power pondered the issue they saw as a threat to the natural order of society.

'Aye, we know about men like Lilburne and Winstanley, but what about those below them who recruit others to their cause?' Jonathan Marlow asked.

'We need to lance the boil that is feeding sedition and heresy to ordinary folk. We must remove those at the head of the serpent and the servants who spread their poison,' Sir Charles said, looking up and staring into the fire.

'How do we find and identify such men, Sir Charles? Where are these men like Lilburne and Winstanley preaching their sedition and heresy?' Paul asked, and again there was a pause in the conversation as each one of the five gave the question some thought.

'They meet in taverns and inns, where the landlord is likely to be sympathetic to their cause,' Sir Charles said.

'But which taverns, Sir Charles? There are hundreds in London alone. If we went to each one with armed guards any meeting would quickly evaporate, becoming no more than a busy hostelry.' James said.

'Aye,' Jonathan added, 'and if they meet where the landlord is of the same mind as them, he is not likely to tell us who they are, or when they meet.'

'Any man will talk if they are stretched on the rack,' Paul Gooding said, referring to the usual instrument of torture for gaining a confession.

'I think we can be more clever in establishing who they are, Paul,' Sir Charles replied, 'we can use the rack later once they have been arrested. All we need is one man to infiltrate one of their meetings and to become part of their web. I think he would soon learn of where, when and who.'

'Ah, yes, Sir Charles. I see, we need a spy in their camp. Do you have someone in mind?' Jonathan asked.

'Better than that, Jonathan. I have someone making discreet enquiries in his regiment amongst men who are known to express disquiet. But it has to be done gradually to gain the confidence of soldiers, lest they become suspicious. He is a young officer and has been laying the groundwork by listening to men and showing a sympathetic ear, even expressing his own dissatisfaction with Parliament,' Sir Charles explained.

'Who is this young officer doing such important work, Sir Charles? I would like to thank him,' Simon said with a smile.

'As would many men like ourselves, Simon. But please be patient and understand his identity should be kept confidential if our venture is to be successful. I am sure I can trust you but if his identity was to become known it would jeopardise our ambitions and probably his safety,' Sir Charles replied.

'Although we would like to clear up this nest of vipers sooner rather than later, we will have to wait a while longer. Once my man has the information we require, we will strike. The laws of sedition and heresy are clear, and these men will fall foul of them, I promise you. Then the rack and gallows will be busy, and we will purge England of this poison,' Sir Charles said and emptied his glass of port down his throat. 'Gentlemen, please forgive me, your glasses are empty,' and he stood to fill them.

'Thank you, Sir Charles, for your reassurance that there are good men in Parliament who will stop this madness, and for your very fine port,' Paul Gooding said.

'Indeed!' Simon Riches echoed, raising his glass.

Thirty minutes later the four visitors left Sir Charles' private quarters after further reassurance and some more convivial conversation about hunting in their respective counties. After they had closed the door behind them, Sir Charles sat down at the table with his quill. *'Captain Popejoy, Would you kindly come to see me at your earliest convenience…'* he wrote. 'I must get this to the good captain in the morning,' he thought to himself, poured another glass of port and settled into one of the large leather chairs.

February 1653

Michael Martin wrapped the printed sheets in sackcloth, tying
the two parcels secure with strong cord. It would not do for
the sheets to fall out, allowing a passer-by to see the contents
inside. Jeremy Odlin would soon be along with two horses
to transport the two parcels down Barnet Hill into London,
to meet David Davies and Gavin Evans at Holborn. The two
parcels were hidden amongst several other parcels to provide
some anonymity, and would be loaded together onto the back
of one of Jeremy's horses. A short time later there was a knock
on the door of his workshop.

'Good day, Michael,' Jeremy called clearly, trying to
disguise his nervousness.

'Good day to you, friend,' Michael replied as Jeremy
closed the door, providing some privacy. Jeremy's nervousness
was shared by Michael, although there was a small degree of
relief that the petition documents he had printed for their cause
would be leaving his premises. But despite being rid of them,
he still felt concern for his friend. 'God's speed and please be
safe, good friend,' he said as he handed one of the two parcels
to Jeremy. 'Let me help you,' he added as they turned to the
door, beyond which the two horses waited. Once the parcels
were secured alongside six other items requiring transport to
London, Jeremy turned to his friend and held out his hand.

'Thank you, Michael. I will make haste, complete our
contribution to the greater cause, and return tomorrow.' They
shook hands without excessive display, keeping their parting
business-like lest they were seen. Jeremy climbed his horse,
tipped his hat respectfully, took the reins of the pack horse and
made his way out onto Barnet Hill, where he turned south and
made his way downhill at a steady trot.

The twelve miles would take Jeremy and the two
horses about two hours, depending on how long he stopped to
water the two beasts. He had no need of sustenance for himself

having taken some refreshment before going to Michael's workshop, and he knew he would enjoy supper with friends in the Swan Inn in Holborn, just outside the city wall of London.

It was still winter, but the afternoon sunlight was pleasant as Jeremy made his way along the Great North Road, passing villages and hamlets. The first was Whetstone from where his wife, Jane, came from to live with him at the top of Barnet Hill. Totteridge Lane was passed to his right, leading westward to Edgeware. Other roads were marked with signs to Finchley and Muswell Hill, before he got to Highgate, which like Barnet sat at the top of a steep hill. There he stopped, allowing the two horses to drink from a stone trough and eat some grass to the side of the road. As they did Jeremy could stand, stretching his back after an hour in the saddle, and gaze down the hill. On a day of sunshine, he could see densely packed spires, the unmistakeable profile of a great city, where hundreds of thousands lived cheek by jowl, so many that each parish required many churches. There was no-one for him to speak to, but he found himself muttering aloud, 'There it is, boys. London,' but the horses didn't reply, preferring to continue with their refreshment. Once they were satiated, Jeremy climbed up onto his horse and they made their way down the steep hill of Highgate, where at the bottom it flattened out and the Great North Road was known as the Hollow Way, and made its way in a straight line south to Highbury. Along this main thoroughfare into London the traffic increased as it was joined by other roads, and Jeremy found himself following other men on horseback, carts carrying tradesmen and their wares, fruit and vegetables heading for Covent Garden Market, smoked meat for Smithfield Market, and some grand carriages carrying men and women of nobility and wealth. At Highbury the road forked, with one branch heading south-eastwards towards the Tower, the other continuing southwards towards the Strand, before which Jeremy would reach his destination, Holborn.

Finally, just two hours after leaving Michael's

workshop, Jeremy and the two horses reached Smithfield Market and it was a short distance along Cow Lane, so-named after all the beasts that made their way to slaughter at the market, then they turned onto Holborn, the wide road after which the London district was named. His rendezvous, the Swan Inn, was not on the road itself, but set back and accessed down an alleyway. Fortunately, the proprietor of the Swan Inn had erected a simple wooden sign with its name and an arrow directing anyone who was not local to where there was refreshment and accommodation. As Jeremy made his way slowly along the narrow alleyway he was overpowered by the stench of the city and all its different aromas, but most of all the human waste that flowed through the River Fleet and into the Thames, just yards away from the buildings amongst which he found himself. The alleyway led to an open space in which the Swan Inn was located and thankfully the stomach-churning stench of the Fleet seemed to fade. There below the sign above the doorway of the Swan stood the familiar forms of David Davies and Gavin Evans.

'Good evening to you, sir. Have you travelled far?' David called out as the man astride one horse and leading another approached and finally came to a halt.

'Good evening, sir. I have journeyed from Hertfordshire, but it was a pleasant ride,' Jeremy replied. He climbed down from his horse and tied the two sets of reins to a post. 'Would it be possible to lodge here this night?' he asked, continuing the conversation as if it was with someone he was meeting for the first time.

'I believe there are rooms available this night, sir, if you need to rest,' Gavin added to the conversation.

It had been agreed their meeting on Jeremy's arrival would be conducted thus until they were in the safety of the Inn, where they would be free to speak more openly, albeit with caution if persons they did not know were close. But the truth of it was that the Swan Inn was frequented largely by men who shared the same desire for change. John Lilburne himself was known well by the landlord of the Inn, although this was not spread as common knowledge beyond its walls for fear of drawing unwanted attention from the servants of those in power.

'Let me help you with your load, friend. It would be mistaken to leave those parcels on the horse for more than a minute in this district of London,' Gavin said.

Jeremy glanced around to see the walls and corners of the surrounding buildings provided shadows in which he could just identify human forms, although whether they were thieves, ruffians, or just the destitute poor, he could not tell, as the shadows overpowered the light. But he was not about to argue with the advice offered by the Welshman.

'Thank you, friend. What about the horses?' Jeremy replied. 'I will take them around the back, where they can be watered, fed and secured for the night in the Swan's stable. They will be safe there,' David offered.

Jeremy joined Gavin in taking the eight parcels into the Inn, as David led the two horses around the back for a well-deserved rest.

Once inside the Swan, Gavin could relax and the formality of their conversation outside was dropped. 'Jeremy, dear friend, it is a great relief to have you safely here. Let's take these upstairs to your room, where they will be secure. Two to three hours in the saddle will leave you tired and hungry, so we should eat,' the Welshman said.

'Thank you, Gavin. I am fine as the journey was not long and largely downhill,' the Hertfordshire man replied with a smile, relieved to be off the road with his dangerous load.

They deposited the parcels upstairs under the wooden framed bed Jeremy would sleep on that night. The room was locked with a key, and they returned to the main room of the Inn, where after a couple of minutes they were joined by the second Welshman. 'Your horses are settled and will be guarded by the stable boy. Welcome to London!' David said, giving Jeremy a firm slap on the back.

'Ah, thank you, David. I am glad to see you both and appreciate your hospitality,' Jeremy replied, and he too finally felt like he could relax for the evening.

Glancing around the large room lined with tables and booths that offered patrons some privacy, Jeremy could see the Swan was largely populated with men of an age and appearance that would be consistent with former soldiers or serving officers. None of them were young, but neither were they old. Several nodded to David and Gavin if their eyes met, but none stared, making the atmosphere feel convivial and secure. David noticed Jeremy's glances towards the different small groups of men in booths and around tables, speaking quietly amongst themselves, there being none of the rowdiness he might have expected in a London hostelry. 'You need not worry, Jeremy. You are among like-minded friends here,' David said with his warm Welsh dialect and a reassuring smile.

They sat down to a supper of beef stew, accompanied by an ale brewed just a mile to the north of Holborn in the district of Islington, where the city merged with fields. Christopher Douglas, the landlord of the Swan, himself a former soldier in Cromwell and Fairfax's New Model Army, took pride in the food served in the Swan and its fine ale. Originally from the East Riding of Yorkshire, though his own paternal grandparents had fled Scotland during the bitter religious strife of the last century, he proudly retained the raw accent. 'Aye, you'll not taste better beef stew south of the River Trent. Nor better ale south of York,' was a familiar mantra to patrons of the Swan, and on that particular evening Jeremy would not offer any argument. Christopher Douglas was of the same political leaning as David and Gavin, an anger burned in his belly over the inequality and injustice of Parliament. 'The bloody fools in Parliament have become obsessed with making the bloody country more godly,' he would announce to those willing to listen. 'But mark my words, lad. This country will flow with blood again if they don't give the ordinary man a bigger share of this new commonwealth!'

Christopher took time to introduce himself to his new guest, enjoying Jeremy's appreciation of the beef stew and ale. He knew this guest from just twelve miles to the north was important, but not the reason why. However, in the name of the cause to create a better England, he didn't need to know and didn't care. He had come to trust David and Gavin, as the two Welshmen lived nearby and had frequented the Swan for a couple of years. And, perhaps more importantly, he was aware that the two men from west of the Black Mountains were confidantes of John Lilburne, an occasional visitor to the Swan.

After more than five cups of ale, although in truth it could have been more, Jeremy was ready for bed, so he was relieved when he heard Christopher call 'last orders, get you home to bed!' Within ten minutes the Swan was emptied of customers and the door bolted for the night. As a guest staying the night, Jeremy was offered the indulgence of more ale, but he knew the ride back to Barnet would not be pleasant if he continued drinking.

'Thank you, landlord, but I must desist from more ale, lest I am unable to sit upon my horse in the morning.'

'Quite so, very wise Jeremy, tis a pity more do not follow your example, but please call me Christopher.'

Goodnights were said, and Jeremy made his way upstairs to his room for the night. He had made every effort to empty his bladder outside into the conduit that flowed into the River Fleet, when Christopher had announced last orders. Nevertheless, he was glad to see a large pot in the corner of the room illuminated by a lit candle. Holding his own candle, he lifted the pot with his other hand and peered inside to see it was empty, but the ingrained smell of urine told him its purpose. Placing the pot down and his candle on a table, Jeremy employed the pot to relieve himself for what he hoped would be the last time before dawn, and minutes later he was in bed.

Despite the soporific effect of the ale, Jeremy found himself not quite ready for sleep as his thoughts were of the day. 'Have we made a huge error of judgement?' he thought to himself. 'Michael, we may have crossed a line that will lead to regret that we ever met John Lilburne and the Welshmen in the Mitre in October. We are Quakers, Michael,' he thought, 'All we wanted was freedom of conscience, but now we're shoulder to shoulder with men who are demanding more. If this ends badly, we could find our necks being stretched from a gibbet, our bodies left to rot, birds pecking our eyes, to deter others from agitating for change.' As he concluded the conversation with his friend in his head, Jeremy instinctively touched his neck before blowing out the candle, waiting to be enveloped by sleep.

March 1653

Spring flowers lined the road from Ilminster to Honiton, adding to William Fogg's feeling of optimism, returning after three months since staying overnight in the home of Jonathan Bounty. Not a day had passed without him thinking about Susan and the connection he had made with her. She could fill his thoughts for hours and the excitement he felt when he had caught her as she stumbled towards the fire and held her in his arms, and then later after dinner when he kissed her hand, was still fresh in his mind. He wanted more, more of the brief moment they shared, and a more intense intimacy. The puzzle was how he should go about achieving this ambition?

The long drag up Fosse Way towards the church at the top of the hill was becoming familiar to Jessie and Mabel pulling the cart, which as usual was laden with cloth Jonathan Bounty might be interested in seeing. William was also armed with a selection of tales and information about the industry in the south-west of England, knowing these would gain favour with the head of the family. He wondered if he might again be invited to stay overnight in the Bounty home, which could be gratifying in more ways than one. Reflecting on the good fortune that resulted from him getting drenched by freezing rain in December, he had been made welcome by Jonathan and Anne, but more importantly, he had formed a relationship with Susan that made his heart race. 'What are your thoughts and feelings, Susan?' he said to himself, there being no one but Jessie and Mabel to hear. 'Did you write a letter?' he asked, and Mabel's ear pricked at the sound of her master's voice, but there was no accompanying shake of the reins, so she and Jessie proceeded up the hill at the same leisurely pace.

'Jonathan, here is William Fogg!' Anne called to her husband as Jessie and Mabel came to a halt outside the shop on Carders Lane, just off Honiton High Street. Within minutes the two horses were being led to the back of the Bounty family's shop and home, to Jonathan's small stable, which was becoming as familiar to them as inside the house was to their master.

'I am on my way to Exeter and thought I would stop to say hello, Jonathan,' William said as he secured the horses. 'But I will not tarry too long, as I need to get there before late afternoon.'

'What?' Jonathan replied, 'Anne and the children will be disappointed if you do not stay for supper. Besides, we are cheaper than any inn keeper for food and board.'

'You are most kind, Jonathan, but I do not wish to...'

'Nonsense, William, we enjoy your company. Come and have a cup of cider,' Jonathan said, concluding the matter, and led his guest back into the house.

His wares secured in the back room of the shop, William could relax for the afternoon and evening, which was made more pleasant by the presence of Susan. On first seeing him, she blushed as she smiled, looking down rather than allowing her eyes to directly meet his. Only when neither of her parents were looking could she gaze into his eyes, and William felt a thrill as he could see in her face her pleasure at seeing him.

'Susan, I must check the food. Would you kindly get some clean linen for the bed and take William's bag to his sleeping space,' Anne said to her daughter.

'Yes, mother,' Susan replied and gathered an armful of sheets and covers for the pillows from a large cupboard at the back of the living room. Balancing them over one arm, she then leaned forward to lift William's bag, but it was with difficulty.

'Please allow me to help,' William said as he got up from the large chair and moved to assist her.

'Ah, thank you, William,' Anne said, seeing her daughter was struggling. 'Please excuse me,' she said as she turned towards the kitchen.

William followed Susan down the stairs without saying

a word, using the time to admire her from behind. He wanted to wrap his arms around her waist and pull her close, but he knew he would have to treat her differently to the older women he had come to know on his travels, women more experienced in the ways of the world, who he might have enjoyed if he was staying in one of several Devon towns. Once pleasantries had been exchanged, such women knew what he wanted and needed from them, for which they would be rewarded. He liked to think they enjoyed his carnal skills, but in truth, it did not matter as he was paying for them to please him. These thoughts passed through his mind quickly as they reached the bottom of the stairs, passing through the shop to the store area where his bed was hidden by a curtain.

'Susan, I should not dwell here too long, but let me look at you before I go upstairs.'

She looked up into his eyes and William could see she was shy but not afraid. He placed her hands in his and raised them to his lips, kissing them gently, and Susan felt a surge of excitement.

'Oh, William, you have been in my thoughts since last time you were here just before Christmas.'

'And you have been in mine, dear sweet girl,' and he leaned forward to kiss her lips for the first time. 'I have been waiting for this moment, you are truly beautiful, and my heart belongs to you,' he said and kissed her lips again. 'But let us be careful, Susan, lest your parents suspect something. Come to me later.'

Susan's head was spinning, but she could not deny him, she wanted to learn more.

'Yes, I will try, William.'

With that William returned through the shop, up the stairs to the living room, his heart pounding.

As on his previous visit, supper was polite and friendly, dominated by Jonathan's curiosity about his competitors in other towns and the general state of the cloth market.

'This war with the Dutch has pushed up the price of

foreign cloth, Jonathan, as fewer merchants are making the crossing for fear of getting entangled in Blake's efforts to dominate the Channel,' William said.

'Aye, you're right, William,' Jonathan replied, 'wars are never good for trades like ours. As if it was not bad enough that we were at war here for almost ten years, just when it seems peace might bring prosperity, we go to war with one of our nearest neighbours across the sea.'

'Indeed, Jonathan, but I think Parliament's argument is that if we do not have control of the Channel, then trade will become more difficult and prices will rise.'

'I see your point, William, we are truly a trading nation that depends on sailing the seas freely,' Jonathan said, and not for the first time was impressed with the knowledge and understanding of commerce and politics displayed by the man he had come to like from Bristol. 'You see much more of these matters living in a major port like Bristol,' he concluded.

Susan had listened carefully, and the analysis of things she did not understand presented William as intelligent and sophisticated, enhancing his gentlemanly attraction. She smiled when, during a pause in the conversation with her father, William was able to glance across at her, and felt a warm feeling when he returned the smile.

'What say you, Susan?' William asked at such a pause.

'Sir, I mean William, I do not know of such matters,' she said modestly, blushing slightly and looked down at the table.

'Forgive me, Susan. I did not wish to cause you embarrassment,' William said, and stretched his leg below the table, gently touching her right foot with his left.

'Oh, thank you William, do not worry, I will be fine,' she replied, looking up and smiling again, as below the table she returned the gesture with her left foot on his right. Not for the first time they both felt a surge of excitement course through their bodies.

As was becoming a tradition during William's visits

he and Jonathan sat in the two large wooden chairs by the fire, which was still being lit most evenings, even if it was the beginning of Spring. Anne and the three children sat on the high-backed bench for a while, until it was time for the two younger siblings, Alice and James, to go to bed. An hour later, after three glasses of brandy, Jonathan decided he too would retire for the night. Anne and Susan had both sipped a glass of the warming spirit, resulting in a happy atmosphere, and William was charmed by Susan's laughter. With the exit of Jonathan, Anne decided it was time for everyone to retire to bed, but like her daughter Anne was also affected by the brandy.

'Susan, I must declare I feel light-headed and do not want to fall down the stairs. Would you kindly show William to his bed and ensure the doors are bolted. Good night and sleep well, William.'

'Thank you, Anne. Good night to you,' he replied as he stood up and bowed politely.

As the door closed behind Anne and they were alone, Susan smiled and walked over to William. 'Well, I had better put you to bed, as my mother has told me,' she said and leaned forward to kiss him on the lips.

'Lead on, sweet girl,' William said.

They both carried a candle in one hand, using the other to hold the bannister as they descended the stairs. But once at the bottom of the stairs, William could not wait any longer.

'Stop, Susan. Wait.' He placed his candle on a table, and once Susan was facing him, he gently took her candle placing it alongside his. Then he folded both arms around her and kissed her first on the lips, then on her neck. Susan responded with a sigh of pleasure and pressed her lips against his. They stayed there for minutes, their bodies joined, both experiencing arousal and desire, but it was not the right time as Susan knew her mother would not yet be asleep.

'William, I cannot stay here too long, it is too great a risk, my love.'

'I know, my darling. Just one more kiss, and know that when I finally fall asleep tonight, you are the last thing I will see, and you will be there in my mind when I awake.'

'As are you to me, my love,' Susan replied.

They shared one more long kiss, their bodies still conjoined, before Susan reluctantly pulled herself away, picked up her candle and left the sleeping space at the back of the shop as silently as she had arrived.

April 1653

'You have sat too long for any good you have done. Come, come, I will put an end to your prating. You are no Parliament. Some of you are drunkards, and some of you are worse. How can you be a Parliament for God's people? Depart, I say, and let us have done with you! In the name of God go!' Oliver Cromwell bellowed.

A member of the Council of State and commander of the army, Cromwell had entered Parliament with a troop of forty soldiers under the command of Charles Worsley and cleared the hall. Stepping across the floor he picked up the ceremonial mace, the symbol of Parliament's power and sovereignty, and passed it to Worsley, his friend and trusted advisor.

'Take this bauble away!' Cromwell spat the words with contempt.

The Rump Parliament, which had sat since the regicide of Charles and the creation of the Commonwealth of England, consisted of about 210 MPs sympathetic to the Parliamentarian cause. Despite passing many laws to set about making England a more godly land, Parliament was seen by the Puritan leader of the army as being populated by the unrighteous. MPs seemed to be sinking into a quagmire of self-interest, not serving and providing a leadership of virtue the country desperately needed. For Cromwell it was not enough that in May 1650 the Adultery Act made incest and adultery punishable by death, and fornication an imprisonable offence. Then in August 1650 the Blasphemy Act was passed to stop the excesses of some religious groups. Former Crown land and church property was seized and sold, raising revenue for Parliament. However, after three years Parliament was not dissolving itself as it had promised. Perhaps their noses were too deep in the trough. 'Have these MPs forgotten why we fought a civil war?' he thought to himself. 'We removed the monarchy because it was not serving the people and now these republican MPs seem mired in self-interest like the rulers who preceded them,' his thoughts continued as he marched out of Parliament into the Spring sunlight.

'Major Flain, walk with me,' Cromwell said to his aide as he marched across the green patch of land that sat in front of Parliament, making his way to the ancient church known simply as the Abbey. It had stood for almost 600 years, for the first 500 of those years housing the dedicated servants of the Catholic Church. It had also seen the coronation of kings and queens, but neither of these outdated institutions would be accommodated any more within its sacred walls.

'Yes, sir. What would you like me to do?'

'Please lend me your ear, Major Flain, and I would beg you to give me your truthful opinion.' Cromwell turned to face the major as he made his plea, which was met with surprise by the young officer, who glanced behind to see if the two guards who followed could hear. He was relieved to see the five paces at which they respectfully followed allowed some privacy.

'Of course, sir. I am here to serve you, in whatever way I can,' Flain replied, wondering what his master would ask.

'War is more straightforward, Major. We prepared ourselves and fought, placing our fate in God's hands. Peace should be easy, but it is not. Parliament has not delivered what it promised in 1648, and it became corrupted by self-interest and intolerance.' Cromwell was facing the great doors to the Abbey as he spoke, knowing the Major would be listening to every word. He liked the young man, who had distinguished himself in the Civil War, Ireland and against the Scots. Any assassin would have difficulty getting past Steven Flain, as well as the usual guards close behind. But it was the temperament of the aide that impressed Cromwell more than his physical prowess. Serious, sincere, modest, spiritual, but tolerant of all Christian denominations. And it was this last quality that he would explore through conversation as they stood for a few minutes in the shadow of the great Abbey, before going in to pray for further guidance.

'Yes, sir. Fighting wars is brutal, but more straightforward. It must be difficult to find consensus in Parliament amongst the representatives of the people we call MPs.' Steven offered a brief opinion, trying to be balanced and fair. He was uncertain where this conversation would lead, and he guessed the general was not likely to react adversely to criticism of MPs and Parliament, but he would still be wise to be careful, not over-reaching himself, or his position. However, he needn't have worried.

'Major Flain, I am pained to see what has become of the republic we all thought could bring about changes for the better. Since 1648 it has become dominated by Presbyterians following the teachings of Calvin, like our cousins from the north.' Cromwell paused, allowing the young major a moment to reply.

'Yes, sir,' Steven replied, beginning to understand where the conversation was going. He had witnessed the division in post-regicide England, leading to a Puritan movement dominated by Presbyterians and their intolerance to other Protestant denominations. This had particularly affected many fellow soldiers, who had fought for Parliament and greater religious freedom.

'I support the need to move towards a more godly society, Major, and passing morality laws may have been justified. But these damn Presbyterians have used the new blasphemy and heresy laws to criminalise half the army, and I cannot stand back and watch anymore.'

'No. sir. I understand and fully agree,' Steven replied. He was being sincere too, having seen the demise of men from his own company, for the crime of being Quakers and Levellers. These men were part of small Christian denominations collectively known as Independents, believing in the same God as all Christians, but with different ideas of how to worship. Quakers' and Levellers' ideas about equality and wealth brought them into conflict with the established rich and powerful men who had dominated Parliament and the army before the war. Now the war was over, their ambitions were at odds with the establishment, who King or not, wanted to see England return to normal, which did not include greater equality or a fairer distribution of wealth.

'My England must be more godly, but it must be fair and tolerant, Major,' Cromwell continued. 'I would like you to tell me how the men in our army feel about the changes of these last four to five years.'

'Sir, I am uncertain of what you would have me speak. I am a soldier and prefer to leave matters of theology to more learned men.' Major Flain felt more comfortable listening to the man who had just closed Parliament, rather than asserting his point of view.

'Come, come, Major. I give you my promise before this church and God. You have nothing to fear. Tell me how the men feel and speak. It saddens me, during these last two years affairs of state have taken me away from the soldiers I cherished as brothers.' Cromwell spoke sincerely, facing the young officer, and for the first time the fifty-four year-old general known as Ironsides looked slightly less fearsome. He was appealing to Steven, possibly lonely, a man in need of a confidante. Steven paused for a moment, collecting his thoughts.

'Well, sir, if I was to speak freely, I would speak of the men and how they feel betrayed by Parliament.' Steven felt emboldened by the invitation he had received.

'Go on, Major. How do you mean, "betrayed?" Is it a matter of religion?'

'Yes, sir. It is concerning religion and the freedom a man might have to choose how he worships God. But it is also about a man's place in society. It is about power as well.'

Cromwell nodded. 'I am listening, Major.'

'Many of us were motivated to fight for the Parliamentarian cause by the changes the army brought. Your New Model Army, sir.' Steven was growing in confidence to express himself but was interrupted by his master.

'Sir Thomas Fairfax, Major! You honour me with such an accolade, but the army was rebuilt by Sir Thomas, not me.' Cromwell felt a return of the regret of the last four years, whenever thoughts of Fairfax were raised, who had lost his heart for the Parliamentarian side after Charles' execution.

'Forgive me, sir.' Steven replied, continuing, 'Yes, Sir Thomas Fairfax was the commander of the army, with you as his second-in-command. But that is pertinent to my point, sir.'

Cromwell listened, intrigued, replying, 'Please continue, Major, and I will try to desist from further interruption until you finish.'

'Sir Thomas Fairfax is a man of the nobility, a Lord, like so many of the leaders, generals and officers in the old army, and those men of power in Parliament. Sir, with respect, you were not born into a position of power. Your origins are relatively modest, a man of land-owning gentry. This was important to the men you commanded, who came to love you, willing to follow you into battle. They could look at you and see one of them.' Steven paused, considering what to say next, wondering how far he could go in expressing discontent within the army.

Cromwell smiled, uttering a simple, 'Aye, thank you, Major.' They both stood looking at the Abbey, and Cromwell found himself thinking, 'Ordinary men rising through the ranks on their merits.' He was liking the young Major more and more.

'It is a sad irony that it took a war to provide men with the opportunity for advancing in society, Major. I saw many of our brothers in the Parliamentarian cause rise from modest backgrounds to be commanders of men,' Cromwell said with some pride, before continuing, 'Colonel Thomas Pride, who led the purge in 1648 was like so many senior officers, whilst not Levellers, who wanted change. They were from lower classes of society than those who came before: Pride had been a drayman at a brewery; Colonel Thomas Harrison was a butcher; Colonel William Goffe was a salter; Lieutenant Colonel John Hewson was a shoemaker; Major Thomas Kelsey a button maker; Colonel John Okey was a tallow-chandler; and Major General James Berry was a clerk to an iron works. I knew all these men, Steven.' Cromwell's use of the Major's Christian name indicated the growing confidence he had in sharing his thoughts with the junior officer. 'But now, it seems these men are dissatisfied with our republic and those men in Parliament we have had to expel today. I hope our actions will go some way to satisfying our brothers in arms, Major.'

'I think it will, sir. Since 1648 there have been so many changes driven through Parliament, which most men in the army can find common ground with. Abolishing bishops and removing the Common Prayer Book were details that did not affect the lives of ordinary folk. Laws punishing adultery, fornication and other immoral behaviour like gambling and drunkenness, were probably long overdue as our country seemed to be heading for hell in a hand cart. But Parliament has not dissolved itself to allow new MPs to be elected, as was promised, and they seem intent on making themselves wealthier. Worse, the new laws punishing blasphemy and heresy, whilst having good intentions, have been used to suppress any independent Christians who prefer to worship God differently. Many of us suspect powerful men are using these laws to crush the demands of Levellers, who seek equality and a fairer share of the commonwealth.' Steven was able to express his earlier thoughts, and drove it home with a stinging comparison, 'Heresy and blasphemy laws are used by the Presbyterians as Italian and Spanish Catholics use the Inquisition!' With that he stopped, his points made, and waited for a response from his master.

Cromwell did not speak for some moments as he pondered, which seemed ages to Steven, then simply said, 'Aye, I think you're right, Major Flain.'

Then he led the young officer through the great door of the Abbey, where they found a wooden pew at which they could kneel and pray. As they got up, Cromwell felt light-headed and nauseous. 'Oh no, not now,' he muttered under his breath.

'Are you unwell, sir?' Steven asked.

'It is not anything to cause alarm, Steven,' Cromwell replied, 'It is a curse I must suffer, but would welcome your escort back to my private quarters.'

'Yes, sir, of course,' Steven said, and they made their way back to the Palace of Westminster.

Fifteen minutes later when Steven left Cromwell in the care of his aide, beads of sweat could be seen on his temple and he appeared to shiver, as if it was winter.

'Thank you, Major. I am in safe hands and this ague will pass. Come back to me tomorrow.'

'Yes, sir,' Steven replied, and made his way back out towards the river, a little concerned, even though he had been made aware of his master's malady some months earlier.

Cromwell knew there was nothing to do but to go to his bed and get through the impending fever, which might last the evening, or possibly through the night.

'I have prepared your bed, sir,' Michael Coleman, his trusted aide, said, fetching a jug of water and clean sheets if they should be required during the night.

'Thank you, Michael,' Cromwell said through a furrowed brow, the sweat spreading from his head to his armpits and back. 'Just get me into bed, and get word to Doctor Wilkins and my wife, if you would be so kind.'

Michael got the fire burning, knowing his master would feel cold chills, then left to deliver his instructions to Doctor Wilkins and Elizabeth Cromwell.

Cromwell was soon writhing under the sheets and blankets, tortured by fever and once asleep by the inevitable dreams. 'The men, guilty of heresy and blasphemy, they will hang for their freedom of conscience. Is it wrong? Parliament and the law must be obeyed. But they are good men. Good men must hang,' he said in a state of delirium. Then he woke, his nightshirt wet, as were the sheets. He looked around the room, still lit by a low candle and the fire, telling him he must have slept for a few hours. Thankfully, the fever had passed but he knew the rest of the night would be more comfortable if covered by dry cloth. Michael had left clean replacements on the shelf above the bed, so he lifted himself up and changed both nightshirt and sheets. 'Dear God,' he said to himself, 'will this malady afflict me until the day I am placed in a wooden box?'

Before sleep came to his rescue, he was able to lay thinking about the dream, which was still vivid. 'Now Parliament and its persecution of good men is giving me nightmares. Where will this end?' he thought, before turning over and closing his eyes.

May 1653

May 1653, Bristol
My dearest Susan

It is with excitement that I write this letter. Although
I am sorry that my work in the summer months dictates me
visiting more towns, resulting in only a few hours in Honiton
on the way to Exeter and further on to Plymouth. Not being
able to stay at your home deeply saddens me.

Susan, I fell in love with you when you almost fell into
the fire in December, and I was able to stop such a calamity by
holding you in my arms. In that brief moment we were together
in a close union, our bodies joined as one. Ever since thoughts
of you have filled my head every day after we agreed to write,
and this was followed by the moments we shared in March.

How are your days? I know you work so hard
supporting your parents in the shop. They are most fortunate to
have such a kind and loving daughter, and if I may be so bold,
one so beautiful. My darling, I have cared for you for a longer
time than you will be aware, admiring your development from
girl to young woman, and it was propriety that stopped me
from expressing this love until you reached womanhood. Now
I find myself drawn to Honiton with regularity because I need
to see you, and my dreams have been realised just knowing
you have affection for me. Kissing you made my heart leap and
your pleasure gives me hope that we can learn more of each
other through closer intimacy.

My heart's desire is for us to be joined as man and
wife, which may not be possible yet, but I believe will be one
day. The law may keep us apart for now, God will not, and
he will grant us our wish to be together. If necessary, I would
leave this life here in England, seeking refuge in the New
World, if it meant we could be together as God wishes. Every
week ships sail from Bristol to the Massachusetts Colony
and I speak to men who describe other parts of the Americas

being settled by men and women seeking a new life. The opportunities there seem boundless and we could be together.

Please forgive me for being so forward and tell me if you wish me to desist. When I go to bed each night, you are there in my mind and in my heart. I long to hold you in my arms, my body aching until our next embrace.
With much love and devotion
William

May 1653, Honiton
Dearest William

Thank you so much for your letter, which I cherish and keep close to me at all times. Each night I read it in bed before sleeping with you in my dreams. Please do not fear being too forward, I am grateful that you have helped me discover emotions I did not know existed. I believe these are true love, feelings and emotions changing me from being a girl to becoming a woman, and I neither think I can, nor desire, to go back. The course is set, and I want you more and more each day. Like you, I long to embrace you, kiss your lips, and much more my love.

Seeing you only briefly these last two visits was painful for me but receiving your letter and writing this to you allows us both to tell the other how we feel, and I feel reassured by your words. Every week I hope my father will say 'William Fogg is intending to call in on his travels through Devon, so get the sleeping space prepared, Susan.' Or, I hope perhaps you are able to visit unannounced and my heart races on seeing you. Then we get to the end of another week and you did not appear, which leaves me feeling sad, but I know I must not be selfish. Please take care on your travels, because my heart could not survive if something happened to you.

If we cannot be man and wife here, I would go with you to the New World to be with you as I believe God intends. This would not be an easy decision, William, I love my parents and my dear sweet brother and sister, but I know I will never *be happy unless I can be with you. At night I think of you and whether I am being sinful in my desires. I feel torn between my emotions for you and what I have been taught as right and proper, so sometimes guilt leaves me feeling melancholy, but I know our desires cannot be denied.*

With much love and longing until we next meet

Susan

June 1653

The Swan Inn in Holborn, London, was crowded with men, some who had been there many times, others who were there for the first time. They gravitated towards groups who were familiar to them, the reason being they shared similar values and had met before. Jeremy Odlin and Michael Martin had just arrived and found themselves in a corner where Michael could stand without bending his neck. They had come at the invitation of David Davies and Gavin Evans, who thought they would benefit from meeting men of common aims. It was Gavin who saw them in the busy inn, Michael's head being easily seen above the crowd. Squeezing between the different groups, Gavin led David, each holding two cups of ale, to the two men from Barnet.

'Good day to you both,' Gavin said, 'It is most opportune that you have both come today,' and he handed Jeremy and Michael each a cup of ale, 'as you will see there are men from different backgrounds sharing common ambitions.'

'Thank you, Gavin,' Michael said nervously, still uncertain whether he and Jeremy had made the right decision in journeying south from Barnet to attend the meeting. But, partly reassured by Jeremy who had made the journey four months earlier to deliver the petition he had printed, Michael had joined his friend on the two hours horse ride.

The conversations of the numerous groups gathered in the Swan created a noise making it difficult to hear each other without either shouting or being so close they might easily make physical contact. However, above the sound of scores of voices, a call was heard appealing for order.

'Brothers! Welcome to you all!' It was Christopher Douglas, the proprietor of the Swan, and the noise died down until there was quiet. Douglas was able to modulate his voice but was still required to project it to all corners of the inn. 'We are all here because of our common dissatisfaction. You may be from different groups. You may have been members of groups that no longer exist. Perhaps they were oppressed by the government and the church. Or you may be new to the dissenting movement. It doesn't matter whether you were a Digger, Leveller, Ranter, or Quaker, we are here as one movement demanding freedom and justice,' the landlord of the Swan announced.

The audience had gone quiet, but there were murmurs, as men were uncertain about being described as being part of 'one movement.' Quakers like Jeremy and Michael generally had not agreed with the more extreme demands of the Diggers, with their calls for land. Was it any wonder they had been crushed by Cromwell in 1650? Now the remnants of that movement were joining the Quakers. The same applied to the Levellers, who had also been closed down by the army under the orders of Parliament.

'Friends,' Douglas continued, 'we need to work together to achieve our common goals. We are stronger together!' His call was met with a general nodding of heads, with a few calling out, 'Aye.' The landlord of the Swan had brought the gathering to order and then he handed over to the two men to whom most had come to listen. 'I would bid you listen to two men here who know more about the struggle of dissenters than most. They are John Lilburne and Gerrard Winstanley!' With that, Christopher Douglas stepped down from the chair, to be replaced by Lilburne, who was joined by Winstanley standing on an adjacent chair. There was applause by most, with a few cheers, but there was also a quieter reception from some like Jeremy and Michael, but everyone was there to listen.

Lilburne spoke first, followed by Winstanley. Both men had learnt to ameliorate their arguments for change, particularly Winstanley, who no longer demanded land reform. Instead they focused on freedom of conscience and the election of MPs. They shared the platform, speaking in turn to press home their views about the church and Parliament.

'For 600 years since we were conquered by the Normans and they imposed on us a system of feudalism, we have been oppressed and exploited,' Gerrard Winstanley said to the audience, before continuing, 'and the church has been a crucial part of that system.'

As the widely recognised more radical dissenter spoke, some in the audience felt unease. The desire for freedom of worship that virtually everyone wanted was not something they necessarily attached to the Norman Conquest, feudalism and the church. Lilburne could sense the doubt, realising his fellow-speaker's points required clarification.

'The Reformation was started by Luther because of the greed and corruption of the Catholic Church, with indulgences allowing a wealthy man to buy his way into heaven. The tragedy is these last 100 years, the Church of England has continued to fleece people of their money, not just the rich man through indulgences,' Lilburne said, and murmurs spread as he struck upon a common anticlerical sentiment amongst dissenters of all shades. He felt the audience's sympathy grow.

'The Church of England is still very wealthy, its unelected ministers living in comfort, provided by the tithes we all pay,' Lilburne added, and the crowd warmed to what they were hearing.

'Aye, that be right, the church grows richer, while we grow poorer!' and, 'Freeborn John speaks the truth!' were comments that encouraged Winstanley to feel emboldened to add more.

'Friends, the church and priests lay claim to heaven after they are dead, and yet they require heaven in this world too, grumbling mightily about people who object to paying tithes to fund them, saying the poor should be content with their poverty, and they shall have their heaven later!' Winstanley said, raising his voice. 'Men gaze up to the heavens, imagining their happiness once they are dead, or fearing hell. Well, why can't we enjoy some heaven here on earth, instead of the hell brought through the misery of poverty!' Suddenly, most of the audience was behind Gerrard Winstanley, as well as John Lilburne, the two orators offering convincing arguments, secretly harboured by thousands.

'Heaven and hell are not waiting for us after death!' Winstanly announced. 'They are here on earth!' And there it was, the statement few would dare speak. The promise and threat of a thousand years, taken from the Bible by the church and priests, was being denied. Was it all a lie, perpetrated by those with power to control the people, a central premise in the natural order, along with other controls like feudal masters and serfs?

'Why are we accepting church ministers we have not elected, and then expected to pay for them?' Lilburne added. 'They should be elected by us, the people, just as we should be electing our MPs, rather than it being left to land and property owners!' He joined Winstanley in spelling out for the dissenters what they should be demanding.

Feeding on the rising tide of support and the oratory of Lilburne and Winstanley, as well as cups of ale, more members of the audience called out and cheered in support of the message, until the inn was filled with a cacophony of sound. Even Jeremy and the unsure Michael were nodding their heads in agreement, the words they heard so convincing. However, in the crowd there were two who smiled and nodded, to not appear suspicious, but they were listening for different reasons to the rest of the throng inside the Swan. Steven Flain was in one corner, making mental notes of what was said and the comments of the audience. He wanted to accurately relay back to Cromwell everything he heard, particularly the emotions of so many former soldiers. But the young major was not to know there was another officer in civilian clothes close to the door. Captain James Popejoy had heard enough, and was one of the first to leave, hurrying back to his lodgings near St Pauls to make notes, before he forgot the details of what he had heard. However, he reported to a different master and for a different purpose. His motives did not include Cromwell and Flain's empathy for dissenting former soldiers, but to identify those same men who might be guilty of heresy and sedition.

Lilburne and Winstanley completed their orations and joined groups of men with cups of ale, willingly clarifying any points and discussing how their proposed changes could be delivered. Jeremy and Michael did not try to get close enough to listen, a difficult task as the two orators were surrounded by listeners. Instead, they found a table vacated by some of those leaving to make their way home to different districts of the great city. Joining them, David and Gavin brought over four more cups of ale.

'What did you think?' Gavin asked with his thick Welsh accent.

Jeremy and Michael looked at each other, expecting the other to speak first, resulting in a pause, so David helped them.

'Was there anything you men of Barnet disagreed with?'

'I think we find their demands reasonable, David,' Jeremy replied, adding, 'it's just that as Quakers we are not so politically vocal.'

'Aye, I can see that,' Gavin said, 'but your desire for freedom of conscience will not be achieved by submissive requests and quiet prayer, my friend.'

Michael nodded, showing he understood, but there was still uncertainty.

'Yes, Gavin, but we must be careful, lest our necks be stretched for heresy and sedition,' the tall printer said.

'Only through solidarity together will we be strong enough to withstand such allegations, Michael,' David said.

Michael nodded his head again, adding, 'Aye, I think you could be right, David.'

The four men concluded their conversation convivially as their cups of ale were emptied. David and Gavin left the Swan, making their way back to their lodgings, leaving Jeremy and Michael to consider privately what they were getting themselves into. They bought two more half cups of ale as they waited for the inn to empty.

'They are good honest men, Jeremy,' Michael said, 'but are they asking for too much? And are they being mindful of how powerful men in Parliament will react?'

'Aye, I understand your concern, Michael. Is it too late for us to step away from this movement?' Jeremy asked.

'I do not know, my friend,' Michael replied, and they both thought about the future as they finished their ale before retiring to their room upstairs to hopefully sleep well.

Sleeping soundly would have been unlikely if they had known that just a short distance away Captain Popejoy was adding their names, along with those of David, Gavin and five others to his list. Ascertaining those nine names was easily achieved by simply engaging different men in friendly conversation throughout the evening, and he retired to his bed pleased with his labour that night.

July 1653

Laura Longbow enjoyed visiting her cousin Margaret Baddow in Honiton. Her family was her life, but she would be lying if she did not admit that sometimes life on their farm, almost halfway between Sidmouth and Exeter, could be repetitive. Honiton was only ten miles to the north of Sidmouth, so from their farm it was no more than fifteen miles, which on horseback at a nice steady trot could be achieved in less than two hours. Accompanied by her youngest daughter, Elizabeth, and her eldest son, John, the three of them set off late afternoon in the warm July sunshine. Allowing their horses to drink at every stream along the road, the journey was pleasant, and they arrived at Margaret's home in the early evening, just in time for supper.

The next day Laura wanted to visit the shop of Jonathan and Anne Bounty, who she had come to know over the years from being a regular visitor and purchaser of their wares. It was also an enjoyable visit for Elizabeth, as she had over the years become a friend of Susan Bounty, being no more than a year apart in age. Laura wanted to buy some material to make dresses for the winter, for her two daughters and herself. July was just the right time, allowing her a couple of months to complete the task.

'Good morning to you, Laura, and to you, Elizabeth,' Anne Bounty said with a smile as the visitors entered the shop.

'Good morning, Anne,' Laura replied with a smile, as she and Elizabeth stood at the counter facing Anne.

'By my word, Laura, look at Elizabeth. She is quite the beauty, and you look more like sisters than mother and daughter,' Anne said.

It was true, Elizabeth was blessed with all the beauty her mother possessed. Golden hair, blue eyes and a beautiful smile. And it was also true that Laura, whilst being a mature woman of forty years, and having given birth to four children, she retained her beauty that made her pleasing to the eyes of men and the envy of other women.

'Thank you, Anne, you are kind and generous with your words,' Laura replied, adding, 'But speaking of beauty, where is Susan, your wonderful daughter?'

'I do hope she is in Honiton this weekend, Mrs Bounty,' Elizabeth said with a pretty smile.

'Ah, bless you, Elizabeth. Yes, Susan is here, she is upstairs taking care of our guest. I will call her down, but please, Elizabeth, you must call me Anne.' Moving over to the door at the back of the shop, Anne opened it and called up the stairs. 'Susan! Come down, we have more visitors.'

'Yes, mother, we're coming,' came the reply from upstairs. Within a minute Susan appeared with a beaming smile, followed by a tall handsome man, who was also smiling.

'William was telling me about the ships being unloaded at Bristol, mother and the interesting people who bring silks from the East,' Susan said as she entered the room, but then saw Laura and Elizabeth. 'Oh, Elizabeth, it is wonderful to see you!' she exclaimed.

'For us too, Susan,' Elizabeth replied, 'as visiting you is the highlight of any trip to Honiton.'

'Susan, where are your manners. Are you not going to introduce our guest to our visitors?' Anne said, lightly admonishing her daughter.

'Oh, yes, I apologise. Laura and Elizabeth, this is William Fogg, friend of our family,' Susan said with a smile, blushing slightly.

William stepped forward holding out his hand, which Laura shook, followed by Elizabeth.

'It is very nice to meet you, Mr Fogg,' Laura said.

'I am honoured ma'am,' he replied.

Pleasantries were exchanged and it was agreed they would all have some lunch together upstairs at midday. Until then, Laura and Elizabeth would take some air and visit the Saturday town market.

'Good, I look forward to seeing you at midday, Laura. Susan, I must check upstairs that we have enough cheese, otherwise you can go to the market to buy some. Would you kindly show Laura and Elizabeth out?' Anne said, and without further ceremony she turned and went upstairs.

'Yes, mother,' Susan replied dutifully.

'It has been a pleasure meeting you, Mr Fogg, and I look forward to hearing more over lunch,' Laura said.

'Thank you, Mrs Longbow. The pleasure is all mine,' he replied with a smile and a courteous bow.

'We will see you soon, Elizabeth,' Susan said with a wide smile, as her friend and her mother left.

Just ten steps along the alleyway to the High Street, Laura stopped. 'Oh, Beth, I've forgotten my neck scarf. I think it is on the table. Wait here and I will get it.'

'Shall I go, mother?'

'Bless you. No, I think I know where I left it,' Laura replied and turned back to the shop. The door had not been properly closed, so opening it made no sound, and Laura could see her scarf on the table. She walked lightly and quietly, so no one heard her, but as she picked up her scarf, she heard a light laughter. Intrigued she looked over to the back room where the drapes of cloth were stored, and she was frozen by the sight of Susan stood looking up into the eyes of William Fogg, too close to be considered decent. Worse, he had one hand on her waist, the other hand stroking her hair. She felt a revulsion at the sight of the young woman she had known for years in a situation that a gentleman would never place her. But she did not call out, instead moving out of their eyeline and coughing.

'Hello, do you need assistance,' Susan said instinctively, moving back into the shop.

'It's just me, Susan. I forgot my neck scarf, that is all,' Laura said trying to smile, but failing to do so convincingly and staring at William Fogg. There was an awkward pause, and both Susan and William wondered what Laura might have seen.

'Here it is,' Laura said, holding it up. 'I will be on my way, and see you both shortly,' her stare still fixed on William. Then she turned and left the shop to join Elizabeth.

'Do you think she saw us?' Susan asked, nervously.

'I am not sure, my love,' William replied, 'we will find out later.'

'Oh, William, I am afraid. If Laura saw us and told my parents...' Susan's cheeks lost their colour, turning an ashen pallor.

'There is nothing we can do, sweet girl, do not fear. We can say you felt faint and I held you to stop your fall,' William said and kissed her forehead gently.

As Laura joined Elizabeth, her face told her daughter she was concerned about something.

'Mother, are you well, you look troubled.'

Laura had been looking down at the road, thinking of what she had witnessed and looked up at her daughter.

'I am fine, Elizabeth. There was something I thought I might speak of to Anne. Let us get on with our business and return later,' and she put her arm through Elizabeth's as they made their way out to Honiton High Street. Her face cheered up, but inside she was concerned for Susan and thought about how young women were so vulnerable to the vanity of older men. As she did so, she held her daughter's arm more tightly than normal.

Turning left onto the High Street, the market could be seen on both sides of the wide road. It encroached on the thoroughfare but such was the width of the road there was still space for horses and carts to proceed on their business into and out of the town. It was a picture of commerce and prosperity as crowds gathered at the different stalls to buy meat, vegetables, bread, cheeses, grain, beer, cider, wine, brandy, port, clothing, tools, and almost anything a family might require for making life more comfortable. The sight took Laura's mind from the scene at the Bounty's shop, and for a while she could enjoy the Honiton Market.

'I want to see how the price of beef compares to Exeter, Elizabeth. Would you like to look at the shoes on sale over there?' she said nodding towards a stall just along on the other side of the road.

'Yes, mother. Do you think we might buy some shoes for me and Mary?' Elizabeth said, excited at the prospect.

'Well, perhaps you could look and tell me if there are some at reasonable prices,' Laura said with a smile, knowing Elizabeth would find something. She had discussed such possible purchases with her husband, Callum, before leaving their home, but had chosen to not say anything until they were at the market, lest Elizabeth talked of it for the whole journey and night at cousin Margaret's house.

'Yes, mother,' Elizabeth's smile broadened, realising the prospect of new shoes was a reality, and she turned to cross the road to the shoes and boots stall. She had looked to where the stall was located, but not along the road to see if there was traffic, instead turning to wave to her mother.

'Elizabeth!' Laura screamed, but it was too late, and as the young woman stepped out to cross the road, she did not see the horse trotting along pulling a small cart, on which sat a boy of no more than twelve. It ran into her back, its chest striking her with such force she crashed to the ground. The boy saw Elizabeth at the last second, when it was too late to take evasive action, then tried to stop the horse, pulling the reins with all his might. Elizabeth screamed in pain as she disappeared, first under the legs of the horse, then beneath the cart. Only a small number saw the accident from both sides of Honiton High Street, but the screams of mother and daughter quickly alerted everyone of disaster. The horse could not stop immediately and as it slowed Elizabeth's prostrate body emerged behind the cart. Laura's heart was in her mouth as her daughter at first appeared to be lifeless, but her darkest fear was allayed by movement of a leg and a deep moan.

'Mother, my leg...' Elizabeth said with sorrow and clearly in pain. One of her legs had moved but the other stayed still.

'Elizabeth, my darling,' Laura said with some relief that her daughter was alive, but then concern at what injury she had incurred.

Within seconds a crowd gathered around Elizabeth and someone brought a cushion from a stall. 'Here, Miss, place this under her head, but we must take care to not move her,' a voice said. 'I was a soldier in the army, Miss, and saw many injuries, particularly broken bones, which were made worse by rough handling,' the man added.

'Thank you, sir,' Laura replied, 'yes, I have been told this by surgeons. Oh, Elizabeth, what have you done, and why did you not look,' she said gently holding her daughter's hand.

'I am sorry, mother, I was excited to look at the shoes,' Elizabeth said, and a tear emerged in the corner of her eye, before slowly slipping down her cheek.

Within minutes, John Hilton, the town surgeon, appeared through the crowd and took control of the situation. Just as the former soldier said, John Hilton was careful to first establish the injury and then to move Elizabeth with great care. Almost miraculously, Elizabeth had been knocked to the ground with force by the horse, who instinctively tried to avoid stamping on her, but had kicked her leg. Along with cuts and bruises, her injury was a fracture to her left leg, which thankfully did not puncture her skin. John Hilton explained that he would secure Elizabeth's leg with sticks and string, hopefully allowing it to set cleanly, and without deformity for the young woman. The choice they had was whether to move her into a cart in which she could lay comfortably, taking her to Margaret's house to rest before proceeding back to their home days later. Or, they could make her as comfortable as possible and return home that same day.

'Which choice would you recommend, Doctor Hilton?' Laura asked.

'If you have a surgeon where you live, in whom you have confidence, I think I would get her home, where she can rest and mend without further movement. Getting her into the cart now, then out into your cousin's house, then back into the cart days later, is more movement than is desirable. So, it was agreed, Elizabeth was kept as comfortable as possible laying in the road, while Margaret was sent for, along with her cart and Laura's horses. A bed of hay and blankets was prepared and six men, directed by Doctor Hilton, lifted Elizabeth carefully into the cart.

It was still not yet midday, so there was plenty of time to make the return journey fifteen miles to their farm. The thick layer of hay would hopefully prevent any jolts from the uneven road causing Elizabeth discomfort, and Doctor Hilton carefully shaped the hay and blankets to ensure her injured leg was raised, avoiding it bearing any weight. Laura told her son, John, to ride home on one of Margaret's best horses to tell his father and to prepare for their arrival.

Just an hour after leaving Jonathan Bounty's shop, Laura thanked Doctor Hilton and the soldier, whose name she never learnt, hugged her cousin and turned to her daughter. 'Well, Elizabeth, let us get you home.' Taking the reins, Laura gave them a light shake and let the two horses pull the cart up the hill, past Carders Lane on the right, and onwards towards the church at the top of the hill. It was only as they passed by the small lane down which the Bounty family's shop was located that Laura remembered what she saw in the back room. Elizabeth noticed her mother looking over towards Carders Lane.

'Is everything well, mother?' she asked, sensing something was amiss.

'I wanted to speak to Susan and Anne,' Laura replied.

'Oh, I am sorry, mother. I have prevented that.'

'Do not worry, my love. You have done no wrong,' Laura said and wondered if that would apply to Susan and William Fogg. But there was nothing she could do now, just hope Susan will be safe and not make any serious mistakes.

Word eventually reached Jonathan Bounty's shop when

Margaret Baddow called in to explain the sudden departure of Laura and Elizabeth.

'Oh, the poor girl,' Anne Bounty said, to which her husband gave an agreeing nod. There was a general sadness amongst the Bounty family that their friends from near Sidmouth would not be with them that evening, as well as concern for Elizabeth's recovery. A deformity and limp were the last things a young woman of eighteen years needed.

This concern for her friend was shared by Susan, but she also felt a conflicting emotion, one of relief that she would not have to face Laura, her mother's friend, whom she feared had witnessed her moment of intimacy with William. The Bounty family and William had gathered in the shop to listen to Margaret explain what had happened. Anne and Jonathan were facing Margaret, their arms around the shoulders of their two younger children, with Susan and William stood behind them. As they listened to Margaret, Susan felt William's finger gently move down her back, arousing further feelings inside her. No one could see and William was able to continue exploring her body's shape with his fingers, encouraged by Susan's willingness to stand and allow his discovery. Through her body rushed a warm sensual sensation, which combined with excitement at the risk they were taking, made her feel she was losing all reason and control. 'Am I being sinful in wanting him?' she thought to herself. 'I know I am, but I cannot help myself,' she thought, and closed her eyes for a moment as William's hand and fingers moved down from her back to rest at her cheek, which he slowly and gently gripped with one hand. For a moment she felt light-headed, a little confused, her forbidden heart racing like a herd of wild horses. Unbridled passion within wrestled and opposed all sense of duty and reason. It was a relief that Margaret brought the gathering to a conclusion by saying she had to return to her house, and they all set to making preparations for supper.

It was a warm July late afternoon, so Anne told Susan to take William and her younger brother and sister for a walk before supper.

'It is too fine a day to stay indoors, Susan,' her mother said, 'take William, Alice and James for a walk, perhaps down to the river.'

'Yes, mother,' Susan dutifully replied, welcoming the opportunity to be with and speak to William. She knew that they would walk closely with Alice and James initially, but once they were on the meadows beside the River Otter, her young siblings would run off to amuse themselves along the riverbank and in the woods.

A short while later they had dropped down from Honiton High Street, along Clapper Lane and across the meadows. As expected, Alice and James ran across the green field, the grass kept short by grazing cows and sheep. Within seconds they were far enough from Susan and William, allowing them to speak freely. William stopped to face Susan.

'My love, I find it impossible to stop myself from holding you. You fill my heart and thoughts, day and night.' He was looking directly into her eyes, barely a respectable distance from her lips.

'Yes, my love, as I do to you,' she replied, 'but we must be careful, even here,' and she glanced around to see if anyone else was out walking, and then over to the river where Alice and James played a game of chase.

'Indeed, please forgive me for being so forward, Susan. Let us proceed with caution, but before we do, allow me one kiss,' and with that he moved close kissing her lips softly, then stepped back. Susan looked at him and smiled. They were stood beneath the branches of a large oak tree, giving them some protection.

'Let us walk this way towards the woods,' she said, taking his hand for a moment to guide him along the River Otter, before releasing it to maintain a picture of respectability.

As they walked upstream along the riverbank, William saw a wooded area offering some privacy, but they still had Alice and James to think of. Much younger than Susan, Alice aged thirteen years and James just eleven, were full of energy and whilst they could entertain themselves by the river, they could not be relied on to not disturb the privacy Susan and William sought. At the edge of the wood, they all stopped, and William had an idea.

'So, tell me Alice, who wins a footrace between you and James?' he asked.

'Me, of course!' Alice replied loudly with a big smile.

'No, I would, every time,' was John's riposte with an equally wide smile.

Susan smiled, realising William's ploy.

'They are both swift, William. I do not know who would win,' she said.

'Me!' John exclaimed.

'Well, there is only one way to settle this,' William said, 'a fair race right here.'

'Yes, a race right now!' Alice added.

'And to make it memorable, I will give the victor a penny,' William said, pulling a coin from his pocket. 'But where should they race, Susan?' he asked.

'I would say from here to the large oak tree, around which they must run, and back to here, where we will be waiting,' Susan decided.

They all looked back downstream to the tree close to the riverbank. It was probably 350 yards, so there and back would take the two children about three minutes. William looked at Susan and smiled, which she returned. Alice and John handed their light summer coats to Susan and readied themselves for the race, both eager to win the prize.

'Now, this race must be won fairly, no cheating or fighting,' William said with an official tone. 'Is that clear?'

'Yes,' the two competitors replied.

'Very well, do not forget to go around the oak tree. Failure to do so results in forfeit of the race and prize,' the race official said.

'Prepare yourselves…Go!' William said with a raised

voice and the two siblings took flight downstream towards the large oak.

They stood watching for a few seconds as the two competitors ran away from them, then William took Susan's hands gently in his and said, 'Come, my love,' leading her willingly into the wood. There was no need to take more than ten steps before they were hidden from view but could still see downstream the oak tree to which Alice and James headed. They had perhaps two minutes before they must greet the race victor.

'Susan, my darling,' and he kissed her gently, with one arm around her waist, the other at her side with his hand rising to touch her breast. Susan said nothing, allowing him to lead her, which she found intoxicating. She moved her head back so she could look into his eyes for a moment, then pressed her lips more forcefully against his, her passion and desire made clear. William was taken aback for a moment at her response but was pleased with the consent she was showing. There was no time to go much further, but in the minute they had remaining he continued with their embrace, kissing her passionately, and then lowered his hand from her breast to press it against the forbidden area at the top of her legs, producing a groan of pleasure from Susan.

'My love, come to me tonight,' he said.

'Yes, my love, I will,' Susan replied, and she knew it did not matter what might happen, she must go to him.

Their intimacy amongst the trees was interrupted as Alice and James were running back from the oak tree and so they stepped out as the race had only 100 yards to the finish. As the two children came to where their sister stood, it was clear Alice would win and James stopped short of the line, the race lost.

'Well done, Alice, the victor!' William announced. Alice was jubilant, James crestfallen, so walking back William gave him a penny as well, congratulating him for his fine effort.

Fifteen minutes later they were back at the house, and an hour later the five members of the Bounty family and William Fogg sat down to supper. Anne had bought a chicken at the market, which she was assured by the stallholder had its neck snapped just that morning. The roast chicken was accompanied by parsnips, turnip and cabbage, washed down with a fine Devon cider. As ever, Jonathan Bounty led the conversation, engaging William with his thoughts on the usual subjects of trade and politics, which the latter tried his best to follow. However, his thoughts were elsewhere, as were Susan's, and they both relived the two minutes in the wood by the river, both wanting more.

'My God, I will risk everything to have her,' William thought as Jonathan was talking about the Dutch wars, and when he glanced at Susan he believed she felt the same, such was her willingness less than two hours earlier. Eventually they were saved by Anne.

'Husband, I think William has heard enough of all this talk of politics. Can we discuss a more convivial subject?'

Jonathan relented and invited William to join him at the large chairs by the fireplace, although there was no need for it to be lit in August. An hour later, after three glasses of port, Jonathan was tired and announced he would retire for the night. Anne and Susan were left sat with William for a short while, until he said he too would go downstairs to his bed at the back of the shop. William was not fatigued, rather he was nervously excited, and only by them all retiring for the night could he realise his desire.

'Susan, off to bed. I will take William downstairs and make sure the doors are bolted,' Anne said. As the matriarch made her way to the door at the top of the stairs, Susan looked at William and smiled. That was all he needed.

'Good night, Susan,' he said.

'Good night, William.'

Downstairs Anne checked the front door was bolted, led William to his sleeping space behind the curtain, checking the back door just yards from where he would sleep.

'Here you are, William. I bid you goodnight and sleep well.'

'Thank you kindly, Anne. I most certainly will. Good night to you.'

Minutes later William was in his bed, waiting. He left his bedside candle burning, so he could see how much time was passing, as well as a light in the dark for Susan.

Upstairs Susan was in her bed, waiting for silence to descend on the house, punctuated by various levels of snoring. She was also thinking about what they were going to do. 'Am I insane taking such a risk?' she wondered. 'Should I stay here, safe in my bed and forget what has happened so far?' These were the rational thoughts of an eighteen year-old woman, but she was in love with the man downstairs and overcome with passionate desires she had never known before. She closed her eyes, wanting to sleep, but it would not come and save her from herself, and she knew she must go to him.

The candle had burnt down to a mark telling him almost an hour had passed, and William was still awake. He did not hear a sound but saw a faint light through the back of the shop, which slowly grew. Susan had descended the stairs barefoot to reduce any chance of sound that might wake the others. She even knew the steps to avoid on the stairs as they creaked. Passing through the shop to the backroom, her concern was stepping on something sharp, but no such hazard appeared. Following the light from his candle, she was finally there at the curtain, behind which she hoped William was still awake.

'William, it is I,' she said just as he drew back the curtain.

'My darling,' was all he said, standing to look at her dressed in no more than a thin linen nightshirt.

'I have come to you,' Susan said placing her candle down on the floor. No more words were said. Behind the curtain on William's bed, Susan Bounty discovered carnal desires and pleasure she had only dared to dream. An hour later she returned to her own bed upstairs as silently as she had left. No longer a maid, she lay in bed awake for a while thinking of the intimate pleasure she had shared with her lover.

August 1653

Harry Clarke had been apprenticed to his uncle, Robert, these last six years. Originally from Essex, having been born in the town of Chelmsford, his father, Henry, had persuaded his wife that their son had better prospects in the great city to the west. So, it was with tearful eyes that his mother, Angela, had waved him off at the age of eleven in 1647. That was two years after Naseby which settled the Civil War, or perhaps more accurately, the first civil war. Charles was defeated but still alive, and it seemed there could be stability and growth. But the foolish king could not accept defeat and his failed efforts to overthrow Parliament could be called the second civil war, ending of course, with his beheading at the end of January 1649. Then his son, employing the support of the Irish and Scots, attempted to fight a third civil war, which was finally crushed by Cromwell and his army at Worcester in September 1651. Henry and Angela Clarke witnessed these wars tearing the country apart, realising London was probably the safest place to be through this turbulent period, with law and order being maintained there more than most other parts of the country.

'He's better off with Robert, my love, rather than here where militias roam who might seize a boy of fourteen or fifteen, taking him without permission from his parents,' Henry said two years ago when the Scots invaded England.

'I know,' Angela replied, 'I fear for the young men of England, as it seems we are destined to be forever at war.' So, whilst they missed their eldest son dearly, they were pleased with his position as an apprentice in London under the watchful eye of his uncle.

Being apprenticed to become a carpenter under the tutelage of his father's brother, Harry was treated firmly, as Robert might deal with any young apprentice, but never cruelly, and his uncle came to love him like the son he never had, having fathered three daughters. Furthermore, the Clarke family was close, and gatherings were regular throughout the year, resulting in Harry seeing his parents and three siblings more than an apprentice might normally expect or hope for.

Now, in August 1653, Harry was seventeen, almost a man, and more importantly a carpenter, proudly carrying the tools of his trade alongside his uncle. Living in a small house just north of Bishopsgate and Bethlem Hospital, Harry had been made comfortable in a room that was no more than a large alcove with a curtain, downstairs at the back of the kitchen. It was a space where a servant might have slept but Harry did not mind as it was always warm being adjacent to the kitchen, and his aunt ensured it was clean with fresh bedding. The two rooms upstairs were where his uncle, aunt and three young cousins slept.

Located not far from the city wall, Robert and Harry were perfectly located to work on buildings in the city itself, and on the constant building of new homes as the city seemed to grow and spread northwards each week.

Robert had served in the parliamentarian army under Fairfax and Cromwell, in the first civil war, and like so many others rejoiced after Naseby. 'Surely King Charles must see he has to be a more reasonable man, and listen to Parliament who represents us, the people!' Robert and a thousand others had said. That was in 1645, and two years later Robert was pleased to be back in London with his family. Harry's schooling had ended when he joined his uncle in 1647, but along with hours spent at Robert's side, observing, carrying, fetching, listening about carpentry, he also got to hear great tales from 1642 to 1645. The story of the war and the events that led to it, were ingrained into Harry's consciousness over the years of his apprenticeship. Fortunately he was fascinated, and as the years passed, Robert's commentary became more detailed and nuanced, telling Harry about not just the battles, but also the aspirations of the men who fought, leading many to join sects calling for greater equality and freedom.

By 1650, when Harry was fourteen years of age, he was able to understand more, leading him to ask, 'what is freedom of conscience, uncle?' Robert paused, carefully placing his coping saw down on the floor. He was using it to cut a fine curve in a door frame, which required his full attention and concentration, any mistake resulting in the door frame having to be replaced at a cost he would prefer to not incur. Answering his nephew's question required a different concentration.

'Well, Harry, that would be a philosophical question, which perhaps should be asked of a more learned man than myself,' Robert replied, taking a moment to gather his thoughts and words.

'But I do not think there are learned scholars in this house, Uncle,' the boy said with a cheeky smile, which he knew would amuse his uncle. They both looked about the house they were helping to construct.

'Aye, you could be right there, Harry,' Robert replied, adding, 'although do not suppose all tradesmen are ignorant of serious philosophical matters. I hear John Kesgrave over there preaches at gatherings on a Sunday,' and they both looked over to the man laying a lime plaster over the wattle and daub wall at the end of the room.

'Is he a church minister?' Harry asked, surprised.

'No, he's not a church minister, and that be pertinent to your question, Harry. Freedom of conscience is about a man, or a woman for that matter, being free to worship God as they choose, not being told "you must say this prayer, sing this hymn, do as the church says. Oh, and you must pay the church a tithe, like you and your ancestors have done for centuries." Freedom of conscience is about people choosing to do their religion differently, Harry.'

'Ah,' the boy answered, 'that sounds reasonable to me, uncle.'

'You and me both, Harry. I met a lot of such men in the army. The war has changed things, and many have come to question how we are governed and how we must worship.'

With that, Robert picked up his coping saw and returned his attention to the curve required by the ornate door frame.

Over the subsequent three years Harry learnt more about the sects and each one's demands. As he turned sixteen, he became fascinated by the more extreme groups, like the Diggers and Levellers, and being young the idealism of ideas like common ownership of the land appealed to his innocence in the ways of men. 'Why shouldn't all men own the land equally?' he thought to himself. He respected the modesty and humility of Quakers, but the idea of sitting in a chapel with just God and his thoughts did not excite him in the same way.

Robert did not tell the boy what his own views were in the early years, as it would have been unrealistic to expect an eleven or twelve year old to understand the need for discretion, but by the beginning of 1653, as Harry was turning seventeen, Robert felt he could share more of his sympathies for what each sect argued. However, rather than tell him what he should think, Robert decided to let him listen to the different speakers and decide for himself. 'After all, they are similar in many ways,' Robert thought. So it was that from the Spring of 1653 Harry Clarke started to attend meetings at the Swan Inn. At first, Robert escorted Harry along to the meetings, which he generally found interesting, but he was too old and realistic to consider the more extreme views worthy of consideration, some being clearly laughable. But for seventeen-year-old Harry it was all interesting and exciting.

Over a six month period leading up to August in 1653, Harry heard some of the most famous dissenters in England speak at the Swan. They included John Lilburne, Gerrard Winstanley, and perhaps the most entertaining of all, Laurence Clarkson, whose speeches caused great humour amongst audiences. Clarkson was a leading Ranter, one of the smaller sects who were known for suggesting there was no such thing as sin, which included adultery and fornication. There were stories of Ranters adopting nudity in their gatherings and encouraging sex outside of marriage. Such tales drew audiences to meetings at which Clarkson was rumoured to be speaking, giving rise to great hilarity once men had supped a cup or two of ale.

'Sin was invented by the ruling class to keep the poor in order. It is a product only of the imagination,' Laurence Clarkson announced seriously, standing on a chair.

'Yes, sir. We agree, but perhaps you could explain that to our wives,' a good-natured anonymous voice replied from the crowd, followed by mass laughter as elbows were used to nudge friends and ale was spilt in good humour.

Harry was spell-bound by what he heard, only just seventeen but increasingly aware of the sexual attraction of women. That meeting was in September and he had made his way alone from Bishopsgate along the road named London Wall as it followed the old city wall. He passed by Moorgate and reached Aldersgate, from where his knowledge of the small streets and alleys allowed him to wind his way through to Newgate Street, which he followed to Holborn, eventually turning right onto the small alleyway that led to the Swan.

After the rousing speech by Laurence Clarkson, the raucous audience and a few cups of ale, Harry found himself leaving the Swan later than he had intended and darkness was beginning to envelop the city. He did not get far before he found the ideas propounded by Clarkson presenting themselves to him in physical form, as two women in a doorway saw him approach.

'Oh, look at this one, Lily, what a beautiful boy,' said a woman with a shortened dress revealing stockinged ankles and calves, and a linen blouse that bared her shoulders and cleavage at the top of her chest. She stepped out in front of Harry, who stopped in his tracks, unsure what to say or do. The second woman, dressed in the same manner, stepped out of the doorway and put her arm through his.

'Well, look at you, darling. Why don't you let Kitty and me take care of you? For a shilling we will teach you everything you need to learn to be a man.'

With Lily's arm entwined with his, Harry could have pulled free and run, but something stopped him as he felt a surge of excitement through his body. That was heightened further as Kitty stepped so close to him, he could smell her perfume. A physical sensation swept through his body as she moved her hand slowly down his chest to his stomach, stopping just below his navel. He felt movement in his loins and for a moment he thought he might faint as both women had their hands on him. It was Lily who gently clutched his genitals and his erect manhood.

'Ooh, he's a big boy, Kitty,' she said with a coarse laugh.

'Come on, my lovely. Come with us for a shilling. You know you want to,' Kitty said.

Harry's head was spinning. His cock was telling him one thing, but his conscience said otherwise. He tried to protest but his throat was dry and he stood frozen by his indecision.

'I, I haven't got a shilling...'

But the two ladies of the night were determined to get something from the encounter. 'Well let's see how much you've got and what pleasure it can buy you,' Lily said as she placed her hand into the tunic pockets of the petrified apprentice.

Suddenly a loud voice interrupted the drama in the dark street.

'You women! What in God's name do you think you are doing? Guards, seize them!' A tall man in the clothes of a Puritan pointed at them from twenty paces away and three soldiers moved forward, but Kitty and Lily were alert to the threat.

'Let's be gone, Kitty,' Lily said, and in an instant they disappeared down an adjacent alley.

Harry was panting heavily, clearly shaken by the encounter, which the Puritan interpreted as him being an innocent party.

'Are you hurt, young man?'

'No, sir. I am not hurt,' Harry said unconvincingly.

'Let it be a lesson to you. Aside from immorality and law, if you were intimate with those women you would find it difficult to explain the pox to your bride on your wedding night.'

'Yes, sir. Thank you.'

The tall Puritan left Harry where he stood and followed the three soldiers down the alley in pursuit of Kitty and Lily.

That night Harry wandered back to Bishopsgate avoiding the narrower streets and alleys, where danger might lurk. His aunt was concerned at the late hour of his return and relieved to see him, allowing her to securely lock the door for the night.

'Harry, do be careful, there are dangerous men lurking in alleys and doorways at this late hour,' she said, her concern being cut-throats and thieves.

'Yes, Aunt,' he replied, 'I lost track of the time, and will not stay out so late in future.'

That night in August Harry lay in his bed behind the curtain, thinking about the evening. He thought about the content of Laurence Clarkson's speech and his encounter with the two women. His emotions and physical stirring were still fresh in his mind and about his body. As he lay there he wondered if Mr Clarkson's teachings were either wise, or practical, in a city like London.

September 1653

Captain James Popejoy enjoyed the walk from his lodgings near St Paul's, along Fleet Street, into the wide road called the Strand to Charing Cross, then south down Whitehall and King's Street, arriving at the Palace of Westminster. Everything became more pleasant, from escaping the stench from the small streams and rivers that transferred the city's human waste into the Thames, to the sight of the great buildings of state. The air was cleaner, particularly if the prevailing westerly wind blew, and he thought about what he had been told by a wherryman some months earlier.

'A wealthy man would do well to build his house on the western side of London, sir.'

'Why so, wherryman?' the young officer asked.

'Because the wind blows from the west, sir, so those in the east must smell the stink of other men's shit and dwell in the city's miasma. In the west they breathe the fresh clean air from Buckinghamshire and beyond.'

James smiled to himself as he made his way to Westminster, remembering the lesson told by the wherryman, which was proven to be true on this sunny Autumnal day. Staying almost in the shadow of St Paul's he was never far from the stench of the Fleet River, and as he made his way along the road of the same name the air was more foul than a mile further on, where the Strand reached Charing Cross. He reflected on the importance of the wind, as there were plenty of people in the western half of London producing the waste that ended up in the river, but perhaps they were not housed as densely as in the centre and to the east, where small dwellings and hovels were crammed into the narrow streets. Certainly, there was more green space to the west, Covent Garden just to the north of the Strand being the first, but then just past Charing Cross was the great St James' Park, and green fields appeared just a quarter of a mile to the west and south of the

Abbey and Palace of Westminster. So, it seemed to be true, what the simple wherryman had told him was wisdom.

James was lodging at the house of Mrs Deborah Wolfe close to St Paul's. She kept the title of Mrs, even though she had been a widow for more than ten years, her husband having fallen fighting for Parliament at Naseby. Inheriting his military discipline, Deborah Wolfe stood for no nonsense from her guests, which suited many army officers.

'There will be no women allowed in my house, Captain,' she told James, as she had told a hundred before him.

'Yes, Ma'am,' James replied, relieved that he was not staying in a house of ill-repute, which could be interpreted as suspicious by the likes of Colonel Thomas Harris, a devout Presbyterian.

After laying down the rules of the house, Mrs Wolfe mellowed and showed a warmer side to her nature, providing the young officer with a dry room, clean bedding, and a breakfast of oats and milk.

'Be sure to take care, Captain Popejoy. You would do well to return before dark,' Mrs Wolfe said as he left each day.

'Thank you, Ma'am,' James replied with a tip of his hat.

He had been told to report to his superior officer, Colonel Harris, outside the Palace of Westminster at midday, so he left the lodgings of Deborah Wolfe with plenty of time to spare, knowing that if he was early he could rest for a while watching wherrymen go about their business delivering MPs to and from the Palace of Westminster. This proved to be the case as James arrived at the Palace of Westminster early, so he sat on the terrace that looked down towards the Thames. He enjoyed his career in the army and had survived combat at Worcester, where the Scottish Royalist invasion was defeated. 'Worcester? Imagine if the Scots had won? Would they have got as far as here?' he thought to himself. Now, in peacetime he was doing a different kind of work. Part constable, part spy, investigating dissenters for his senior commander and MPs.

It was not work that came naturally, but he would continue
to follow orders. He was able to stay in lodgings superior to
barracks, and he was exploring the great city. However, despite
this, he still felt a degree of envy watching the wherrymen go
about their business. Theirs was a simple daily toil compared
to his.

'Captain Popejoy!' came a loud call, disturbing James'
thoughts. He looked round to see the familiar face of Colonel
Harris, alongside a man dressed in fine clothes, who wore
polished boots and a well-cut black coat to his knees, below
which were silk stockings. He did not carry a weapon, so was
not a military man. At the top of the coat was a fine lace collar
and cuffs at the end of the arms, as well as a new hat. Before
they reached him and he was introduced, James knew he was
an MP.

'Good day, sir,' James said, jumping up from the table
where he had been sat admiring the wherrymen.

'This is the young officer about whom we spoke, Sir
Charles,' Colonel Harris said.

'Good day to you, Captain Popejoy. I have heard much
about you,' Sir Charles said.

'A knight as well as an MP,' James thought, before
replying, 'Thank you, sir. It is an honour to meet you,' and
gave a respectful bow.

'That's not necessary, Captain. Here, give me your
hand,' Sir Charles said, and they shook hands. 'Let us go to my
private quarters, where we will be able to speak without fear of
anyone listening,' Sir Charles added, and led them past guards
into the building that housed Parliament.

Sir Charles' private quarters inside the Palace were
plush, with elaborate wood carvings adorning the fireplace and
walls. Two large comfortable leather seats were situated just
in front of the fireplace, which was not lit but the hearth was
already stocked with neat piles of wood ready for the colder
weather. There was also a table with two chairs, a washbowl
with a large jug of water, and a curtain across an alcove,

behind which James guessed was a bed.

'Please, gentlemen, sit here,' Sir Charles insisted, gesturing towards the two high backed leather chairs, and he took a chair from the table for himself.

'Thank you, sir,' James said, and as he leaned back, he thought he had never sat in a more comfortable chair.

'Captain Popejoy,' Colonel Harris said, 'I have asked you to come and meet Sir Charles as he and many other members of this house are concerned and very interested to hear about what you have witnessed at the inns and taverns you have attended on our behalf.'

'Yes, sir,' James replied, but that was all.

'Speak freely, Captain. I would like to hear everything, whether you think it is of importance or not,' Sir Charles said, adding, 'Tell us who was there, how many, what was said. Which hostelries have you visited? Are the landlords and proprietors of these places complicit? Anything you can remember, Captain.' There was a pause as Sir Charles and Colonel Harris waited for James to speak. For a moment his throat was dry, but then having composed himself, he took a parchment from inside his tunic and spoke.

'Well, sir, I have been visiting and attending a number of inns and taverns across London for two months now. These are those hostelries known to be frequented by dissenters, which was not difficult to ascertain by listening to conversations amongst my fellow junior officers.'

'Forgive me for interrupting, Captain, but are your fellow officers members of these groups?' Sir Charles asked.

'Not all, sir, but certainly I believe a few are, although they would not openly admit to being so. But ever since the war, these new sects have been swollen in numbers by disaffected army officers and soldiers,' James replied.

The two older men both nodded in understanding and agreement.

'Go on, Captain,' Sir Charles said.

'Over the last two months I have found that the inns

and taverns that seem to attract the most men for the purpose of meetings are the Swan in Holborn, the Three Tuns near Charing Cross, the Mayflower at Rotherhithe, and to the north the Spaniards Inn at Hampstead,' James continued. 'Of those four, I would say the meetings I witnessed at the Swan and the Three Tuns attracted the most men and were the noisiest. Although that may be because they are closer to the centre of London, where there are naturally greater numbers.' He glanced down at his parchment and notes. 'There is usually a speaker, to whom people come to listen, and the two who seem to be most popular are John Lilburne and Gerrard Winstanley.'

'That maniac, Winstanley,' Sir Charles interrupted, glancing at Colonel Harris, adding, 'I thought he and his insane followers, the so-called Diggers, had been crushed in 1650.'

'Aye, we did close them down, Sir Charles,' Harris replied, ''tis a pity we didn't hang him. I understand he has become a Quaker.'

'Has he? Carry on, Captain,' Sir Charles said.

'The inns and taverns usually have a landlord who is sympathetic to the cause they host. At the Swan, Mr Christopher Douglas, spoke to the gathering before Lilburne and Winstanley, making his own contribution. At the Three Tuns, John Wiggett and his niece are not confident speakers like Douglas, but they are friendly with the dissenters and accommodating. I wonder if the young woman earns extra income with the men through the usual means of women who frequent London's inns and taverns?'

'Fornication and whoring, as well as heresy and sedition,' Sir Charles said, with a wry grin, 'the evidence grows.'

'Interesting that Winstanley has emerged in London,' Colonel Harris said, 'the last I heard, he was in Surrey, around Cobham.'

It seems London is the centre to which dissenters of all shades are drawn, sir,' James said. 'At the meetings I attended the air was filled with accents and dialects from all corners of these islands, sir,' he added.

James spoke further, describing everything he saw and heard, referring to his notes. After fifteen minutes he had said everything he could remember or had written down. At the end Sir Charles Hadleigh and Colonel Harris looked at James and each other.

'Captain Popejoy, I would like to thank you for your conscientious work in service of the Commonwealth. What you have told us is valuable information in our fight to stop this sedition and heresy that threatens order,' Sir Charles said.

'Yes, sir,' James replied.

'But the fight is not over, and we need to continue to gather evidence and names, Captain,' the MP added.

Within five minutes, good-byes were said, and Captain James Popejoy had to make his way back towards Mrs Wolfe's lodgings and the miasma of London. It had been a fruitful meeting and he was pleased with how he was received and thanked by Sir Charles. As they left the MP's plush quarters, Sir Charles placed a small pouch in James' hand.

'Please, Captain, this is not a payment, but I wanted to buy you dinner this evening. Alas, I have to go elsewhere, but that should not prevent you from dining well.'

James had looked at Colonel Harris, who nodded his consent.

As he walked towards Whitehall, James paused, took the small pouch from his tunic and checked the contents. Twenty-four pennies. James turned right and made his way down to the river. 'Enough for a pleasant ride in a wherry, as well as supper and some ale,' he thought, before calling out, 'Wherryman, how much to the jetty closest to St Paul's?'

October 1653

The rain fell across London at an angle on a strong westerly wind, from which there would be no escape in an open area like a farm or park. However, walking along the narrow streets and alleys Harry Clarke had learnt that if he walked close to the leeward walls of the largely Tudor buildings, with their overhanging upper floors, he could avoid the worst of the rain. So it was Harry made his way on a wet Saturday evening from Bishopsgate to Holborn, excited to hear another dissenter at the Swan Inn.

Christopher Douglas looked up from behind his bar to see Harry enter the main room. Douglas had been filling three cups with ale from the wooden cask that sat on a platform in the gap in the wall separating the main room from the kitchen. There the cask was safe from being knocked over, only someone behind the bar could access it, and importantly it could sit still allowing sediment to settle so only a clear ale was poured from its tap. Christopher Douglas was proud of the quality of the ale served in the Swan, as were all landlords, a cloudy sediment filled ale tasting less pleasing and more likely to produce 'the runs' amongst customers the next morning.

'Young Harry, come over here, lad,' Douglas called in his strong Yorkshire accent. He had come to know and like the young man who first came to the Swan with his uncle, but these last six months or so often coming alone. 'We are hoping Gerrard Winstanley will be speaking tonight, Harry, so I hope you can tarry a while.' He needn't have worried, it was the possibility of listening to a speaker that had drawn Harry out of a warm dry house into the driving rain that Saturday evening.

'Thank you, Mr Douglas, I look forward to listening to Mr Winstanley and can stay an hour or two,' Harry replied. The experience of two months earlier when he was accosted by two ladies of the night had not discouraged him from going to the Swan, but he was mindful of walking home late. He would keep to the main roads like Cheapside and London Wall, avoiding the small streets and alleyways.

'How is your uncle, Harry, and would you like a cup of ale?'

'My uncle is well, Mr Douglas, and thank you, a cup of ale would be most welcome.'

Harry felt at ease after a few sups of the ale Christopher Douglas poured, and listened to the conversation the landlord enjoyed with two other men.

'Mark my words, John, Parliament will be arresting good men like those in here this evening for crimes of heresy and sedition, just because they want a better life,' Christopher said.

'Aye, the good landlord may be right, Simon. These men in power have no intention of giving the ordinary man greater freedom to have a say in who sits in Parliament, and the church wants to protect its income through tithes, which they lose by allowing greater freedom of conscience,' the third man contributed.

Simon Goodwin nodded in agreement but was struggling to accept Cromwell's Parliament would arrest former soldiers for those crimes mentioned, which could see his former comrades hanging from a gibbet. 'I cannot believe the Lord Protector would let Parliament do that,' he said.

'His hands are tied, Simon. He has to let Parliament execute those laws passed three years ago, lest he risks another civil war,' Christopher said, and Simon nodded again resignedly.

Eventually the meeting got underway as the main room of the Swan filled with a raucous atmosphere. Gerrard Winstanley did not appear, but other men were there, formerly of the Diggers fraternity, who had like so many Levellers chosen to support the growing numbers of Quakers, calling mainly for greater freedom of conscience. But some still demanded more equality through allowing all men to vote for

MPs, and there were still some calls for common ownership of the land. As these demands were made, the noise rose noticeably, the emotions of the audience freed of restraint by the ale. Harry felt the excitement and joined in, cheering and jeering as points for and against the dissenters' ambitions were explained.

'They don't want you to have a vote because they know you will elect one of yourselves to be your MP!' screamed one speaker, and a mass jeering erupted, which Harry joined.

'Why should we pay tithes to the church to keep priests and ministers in comfort, while we struggle to feed our families?' another speaker asked and was answered by an even louder response of jeers.

Finally, the speakers finished, and the crowd began to dissipate. As Harry was finishing his third cup of ale and was thinking about making his way back to Bishopsgate, a young man to his right said, 'They were fine speeches tonight.'

'Aye,' Harry said with a smile and glanced at the man.

'I've been to many of these meetings, but do not recognise you,' the man said.

'I have been coming these last six months or so,' Harry replied, still smiling.

'I enjoy the meetings and noticed you do too,' the man said, with a smile.

'Yes, I do enjoy them,' Harry said, and held out his hand, 'I'm Harry, Harry Clarke.'

'Hello, Harry, it's nice to meet you,' the other man said, shaking his hand. 'I'm James, James Popejoy.'

Five minutes later Harry was walking along Holborn in the direction of Bishopsgate to his uncle's house and his comfortable bed behind the curtain. Within thirty minutes he was in his secure alcove settling down to sleep. As he did so, less than two miles away in Mrs Wolfe's guest house, James Popejoy was adding another name to the list for Sir Charles Hadleigh.

November 1653

Cromwell walked onto the snow-covered terrace outside the Palace of Westminster. It was a bright winter afternoon, and with only a couple of hours until the sun would disappear in the west, he guessed it must be about two in the afternoon. It had been one of those interminable sessions in the Commons, which seemed to go on forever, listening to prating MPs. As Lord Protector he had effectively been ruler of the nation since April, but this did not preclude him from having to listen to those elected representatives of the people. This session did not seem to be about MPs expressing concerns for the people, rather they expressed their concerns about the people, and in particular how the demands of the people were a threat to the property of MPs, their friends and families. He turned to see the welcome sight of Major Steven Flain approaching up the steps that connected the terrace to the road down to the river.

'Good afternoon, Major Flain, I am pleased to see you,' the Lord Protector said with a sigh, which was noticed by the young officer.

'Good afternoon, sir. I trust all is well,' Flain replied, suspecting it was not.

'Thank you for asking, Major, but sadly it is not, and I fear there could be troubling times ahead for us, some of our old comrades, and this house behind us.'

'Sir?'

'I thought we had seen an end to having to suppress the more extreme sects that emerged from the army. But it seems some of the members of this house have intelligence that men who had been Levellers and Diggers are now infiltrating the Quakers and Anabaptists,' Cromwell explained.

Steven Flain knew of such rumours, having listened to fellow officers, but like the man before him, saw no threat. 'We know the Quakers, Anabaptists, and other Christian sects want greater freedom to worship God, but I don't think they are a threat to either government or property, sir.'

'Exactly, Major. You and I can see this, but MPs and their wealthy friends feel threatened.' As Cromwell spoke these words, as if it was a cue on stage, three men approached carrying parchments. Cromwell recognised them immediately, although Flain did not know of them. Sir Charles Hadleigh, Jonathan Marlow and James Banstead were all MPs from the south of England, wealthy landowning men, supporters of the Established Church and fierce opponents of all sects calling for change.

'Sir, Lord Protector, we would beg you tarry a while and listen to our concerns,' Sir Charles Hadleigh said.

'Sir Charles, I have listened to you and an army of MPs for the last four hours. Is it something we did not discuss inside the House?' Cromwell replied, hoping it might be about an innocent, unrelated matter. But he was to be disappointed.

'Sir, it is material to the discussion in the House, which we were not at liberty to disclose for reasons of security,' Hadleigh replied.

'For reasons of security, you say. What reasons of security might they be, Sir Charles?' Cromwell asked, his impatience growing. He had heard enough from Sir Charles and his fellow self-serving MPs, and he was hoping to speak informally to Steven Flain for a short while before attending a prayer meeting, where he might ask the Lord for guidance.

'Should we go somewhere private, sir? On this parchment we have the names of known agitators, who are calling for changes that are both seditious and heretical,' Sir Charles said, glancing at Flain. The inference was clear; could they speak of such matters in the presence of a relatively low-ranking officer in the army, from where so many agitators had come. Cromwell understood their meaning.

'This is Major Flain, with whom I confide and trust, not only with my life, but also the security of the country we hold dear. You can speak openly to me with him present, or you can remain silent.'

The three MPs looked at Flain and nodded to show their respect for Cromwell's instruction.

'Sir, these men are no more than heretics, they are Lollards who would overthrow the natural order,' said Jonathan Marlow, endeavouring to assist Sir Charles in their argument.

'Lollards? Mr Marlow. Are you sure, I thought they all died 250 years ago,' Cromwell quipped, glancing at Flain with a smile. The MP's outrageous remark comparing his soldiers seeking religious freedom to the followers of the priest, John Wycliffe, who questioned the corruption of the Catholic Church more than a hundred years before Luther's protests, caused him to feel some levity. Flain returned the smile, and Cromwell continued, 'Weren't they all burnt at the stake as heretics? Surely, they are all dead, Mr Marlow?'

Marlow blushed, realising his claim that they were Lollards was perhaps not the best one he could have made. 'Indeed, sir. Forgive me, but these agitators are like Lollards in their demands,' Marlow offered.

'What is it that makes them seditious and heretical?' Cromwell asked, the humour in his face disappearing as he realised these men were determined to have his ear on these matters. 'But be warned, gentlemen. I will not have men who are former soldiers, who were willing to lay down their lives for a better England, slandered on hearsay and gossip.'

'Sedition, sir?' James Banstead joined in, continuing with, 'The New Model Army has spawned men who becoming Anabaptists refuse to swear the oath in court, objecting to religious ceremony being used in what they consider a secular judicial process.'

Cromwell listened and paused, Banstead was touching on a legal and theological issue he had considered many times. Could the church and state be separated? Is it possible? Is it right? If our laws are to create a more godly state, can God, through the church, be removed? He understood the aims of the Anabaptists, but he was not about to discuss the matter here with these three, whom he suspected were ungodly whoremongers, motivated by greed and self-interest. At the same time, he recognised the point Banstead was making. Allowing different sects to refuse to comply with the legal process could be deemed seditious.

'Sir, some of these sects question whether there is a heaven or hell!' Sir Charles Hadleigh chimed. 'They say both are here on earth. Heaven is when men laugh and are merry, and when men feel sorrow, grief and pain, it is hell,' he added, causing Cromwell to close his eyes under the strain of listening to their carping. 'Sir, questioning the existence of heaven and hell as taught in the Bible must be heresy!' Hadleigh spouted, raising his voice.

'Sir Charles, perhaps you could lower your voice speaking to our Lord Protector, lest others hear and your request to speak in private is rendered futile,' Steven Flain said, seeing the three MPs were proving painful to Cromwell's ears.

'My apologies to you, sir,' Hadleigh said to Cromwell. 'But these men are dangerous, and you must understand how concerned people are across the country. We urge you, no, beg you to take action, or allow us to take action to stop a revolution that could take us to another, more bloody, civil war.'

Cromwell had opened his eyes, realising this impromptu meeting would not be ended without him addressing their concerns. 'Gentlemen, let me have these names and consider what is to be done. If they are guilty of sedition and heresy, then they must be brought to justice. You have my word.' With that, the three MPs bowed respectfully, and on rising said as one, 'Thank you, sir.' Sir Charles Hadleigh handed Cromwell the parchment, turned and made his way back to the Palace of Westminster followed by his two colleagues.

Cromwell held out the parchment in his hand, offering it to Flain. 'What shall we do with this, Major? It is rare for me to imbibe alcohol so early in the day, but I feel a cup of ale would be welcome.'

'Yes, sir,' Flain replied, somewhat shocked. 'Shall we go back into the Palace to order two cups?'

'No, Major. I have had enough of that place and its inhabitants for one day. Why don't you take me to an inn or tavern, where we might find a private place to sit and talk.' Steven Flain was taken aback, and he was not about to disobey the Lord Protector, but for a moment he had to think of a suitable hostelry. 'Yes, sir. There might be such a place ten minutes from here, where MPs should not be present.'

Major Flain led Oliver Cromwell away from Westminster, followed by his two personal guards, who were dressed in civilian clothes but were armed with swords and daggers. Walking north along the road known as Whitehall, the fresh snow quickly turned to a grey slush, which did not affect them in their polished leather boots but made walking a damp and cold activity for the poor without sturdy footwear. Initially, the man at his side was recognised by people in the vicinity of Westminster, many of them employed by the government, so there were knowing glances and respectful nods. After five minutes they were far enough from the House to be amongst the masses who knew his name but not the face of the Lord Protector. They walked through crowds, rubbing shoulders with men and women of different classes and occupations, until they reached the area of Charing Cross, where Flain paused.

'Are you sure you wish to proceed, sir? We may encounter persons who offend your sensibilities.' Cromwell realised what he might be referring to, as the sight of more men of sinister appearance increased, as well as women dressed in attire less than modest smiling at passers-by. 'Major, I have fought wars. I am aware of the human condition,' Cromwell replied.

The irony did not escape Cromwell that they were in the area where until just five years earlier had stood the great stone cross, a monument to Eleanor, wife of Edward I, one of

England's most powerful kings. His grief at her death more than 350 years earlier, led him to erect twelve such crosses where her body rested on its return to London. This one had been destroyed by Parliamentarians in 1649, in an attempt to remove traces of Royalist memorials. Cromwell wondered if such gestures were a futile attempt to tamper with a nation's collective memory.

'Sir, I believe there might be an appropriate tavern called the Three Tuns along this road,' Major Flain said, and the four men turned down a narrow street. The two guards moved closer to their charge, wary of cut-throats. Perhaps worse, Cromwell and Flain were accosted by women of the night as they passed by doorways, two or three actually touching the shoulder or chest of Cromwell. 'Would sir like some company for the evening?' one asked, to be met by his look of horror and revulsion. 'Suit yerself! He must be one of those Puritans!' the woman said to her colleague with coarse laughter.

Finally, the narrow road opened to a wider space and the Three Tuns sign hung above a door. Steven Flain turned to Cromwell, 'I apologise for the ordeal of getting here, sir, but I am confident we will be safe inside.'

'Very good, Major. Do not fear, I have survived, and the walk was an education. Guards, inside the tavern please allow Major Flain and I some privacy. But be close enough at hand in case we require your assistance.'

'Yes, sir,' the two guards replied, and inside the tavern they sat at a table just five paces from Cromwell and Flain.

'I hope this tavern is appropriate, sir. London inns and taverns can vary in the quality of their ale and food, but also in the quality of their patrons,' Steven said glancing around the main room with its booths and tables. There were several groups in booths, but none either side of the booth Steven chose, offering greater security. In the middle of the room there were six tables, two hosting separate groups of men. Those two tables were eight paces away and the two guards were able to occupy one of the tables closest to Steven's chosen booth. Cromwell scanned the scene and nodded approvingly, 'This is perfect, Major,' and a smile appeared on his face. 'By my word, Steven, no one recognises me.' A feeling of ease moved through his body and he breathed deeply.

'Yes, sir. I think we have the safety of anonymity here,' Steven said, and he realised how oppressive life must be for a man who never finds a place where he is not known. 'Many men in the army would recognise you, along with MPs and officials of state, but it is likely most of the people on this island would not be able to distinguish you from any one of a thousand members of the Puritan gentry.'

'I like that, Major, just a member of the Puritan gentry,' Cromwell smiled, adding, 'I am suddenly hungry, Steven. Shall we eat something, and perhaps try some ale to quench our thirst?' Steven was somewhat surprised at the last suggestion. Drinking ale with the man who hates drunkenness was not what he expected to be doing when he rose that morning, nor any morning. Cromwell could see his surprise and guessed why, so reassured Steven, 'Do not fear, Steven, it is not a trap. I am against drunkenness because it leads to licentiousness, debauchery, profanity and violence. But I do not wish to deny people the opportunity to socialise and enjoy themselves. And I do partake of a glass of wine with dinner, and of course a weak ale is often safer to drink than the local water, depending on the locality.'

Steven nodded, 'Very good, sir. Shall I enquire what food is available at this hour, and order two cups of ale?'

'No, stay seated, Steven. Let me perform that task, as I tire of people waiting on me and would like to meet the landlord,' Cromwell said, causing Steven some discomfort as his master would be beyond his immediate protection for a short but potentially dangerous minute. But there was no time to protest as Cromwell rose from his chair and walked over to the counter of the tavern. As he did so the two guards were startled and watched with some trepidation, but were relieved to see there was no one nearby who could launch an attack without them intervening. However, they both took their hands from the small cups of ale they had purchased, placing them on sword hilts and dagger handles.

At the counter Cromwell was greeted by John Wiggett, the affable landlord of the Three Tuns. 'Good day to you, sir, and what can I get you?' Wiggett had been the proprietor of the Three Tuns for almost twenty years, inheriting it at the age of thirty when his father died in a fight with vagabonds who had attempted to rob the tavern. Before that, John Wiggett had been barman and pot collector, having been born upstairs and lived his whole life in the area known as Charing Cross. Without formal education after the age of nine, John Wiggett prided himself on knowing his letters and words, enabling him to read pamphlets left by patrons, the result being a broad knowledge of different views on politics and religion. He learnt early that being the landlord of a tavern meant it was wise to stay neutral, keeping his personal views to himself, listening and observing those of others. Stood before him was a man of substance, of that he was sure, judging by the quality of his fine lace collar and polished leather boots, and John wondered if the two men sat at the table were connected in some way to this man? 'Yes, you're a man of importance, no doubt,' John thought, but he had no idea that it was the Lord Protector stood the other side of the counter.

'Good day to you, landlord,' Cromwell said. 'Could my friend and I have two modest cups of your finest ale, and may I ask if you could provide us with some food?' he asked politely. John Wiggett was impressed by the manners of the man, not always guaranteed with men of wealth. He served all men the same, whether they be lord or labourer. As long as they behaved themselves and paid without asking for credit, they were welcome in the Three Tuns, and if they could not behave then there was always Betsy, his eighteen-inch club under the counter. But this man of substance was a gentleman.

'Two cups of my best ale coming up, sir, and I do know

we have some beef pie and bread left from lunchtime, if you would care to try?'

'That sounds most appealing, landlord. I am hungry and would like to try your beef pie,' Cromwell replied.

'Have you been busy with work to give you an appetite,' John Wiggett asked, as he would any customer.

'Yes, indeed, landlord. I have worked hard this morning.'

'What kind of labour would that be, sir?' Wiggett asked, continuing the conversation with the intriguing customer.

'I have been...' Cromwell started, then realised he should be circumspect. 'I have had to listen to men complain about their lot and matters of the law, which is both tedious and tiring,' he said, deciding that was all the affable landlord needed to know.

'Ah, the law and men who complain, they be tiring of any man's brain and patience, sir. More tiring than toiling in the field, I would say,' Wiggett said. Cromwell liked the affable landlord, and realised he missed the simple honesty of the working men he knew before 1642, and the soldiers he had known since.

'Joanne Aker!' Wiggett bellowed turning to face the kitchen behind him. 'Two beef pies with bread, woman! There are two gentlemen here in need of sustenance, so get yourself moving! The girl will bring your food, sir,' he said with a smile.

Cromwell returned to the booth with the two cups of ale, placing them down on the table. 'Here you are, Steven, a cup of fine English ale,' he said, and once sat down, raised his cup, 'Thank you, Steven, good health,' pausing as his hand held the cup above the table. Steven was still unsure about drinking ale in a London tavern with the Lord Protector, but composed himself and raised his cup to meet Cromwell's. 'Thank you, sir, good health.'

There was an awkward silence as they sipped their

ale, and Steven felt relieved that it was interrupted by a young woman emerging from behind the counter holding a plate in each hand. As she approached both men glanced over, as did the two guards sat at the table. When she arrived at the booth it was plain to see she was no longer a girl, but still not yet an old maid. Not only that, she was most pleasing on the eye, with a slim figure and long fair braided hair. She wore a skirt that did not touch the floor, but ended halfway between knee and ankle, revealing slim lower legs. Her top covered her arms, but the neckline was low enough to expose her neck and fair skin. Having walked over with a stern face concentrating on not spilling food from the plates, at the booth she was able to smile, revealing fine white teeth, making her even more attractive.

'Here you are, Sirs. Two plates of our best steak pie and freshly baked bread,' Joanne Aker said, carefully placing the plates on the table. Both men took a moment to look at the young woman. Cromwell was first to thank her with a polite nod, followed by Steven, 'Thank you, miss,' and as he spoke he was taken by her beauty. 'You are most welcome, sirs,' she replied with a flash of her pretty smile, and as she walked away, Steven could not prevent his eyes following her feminine form return to the kitchen, which was noticed by Cromwell. 'A most pleasing young woman, Major Flain,' he said with a wry smile, which brought Steven's attention back to the table.

'Yes, sir. Sorry, sir,' he said flustered, causing Cromwell to laugh.

'Do not feel guilt, Steven. There is no crime in admiring the beauty of a woman,' and once again Steven found himself confused by the Puritan head of state.

'Indeed, thank you, sir,' he said, adding, 'She is a fine-looking young woman, and suddenly I too feel hungry.' With that he picked up his spoon in one hand and the chunk of bread in the other, but before he could begin, he was interrupted,

'Major! A pretty woman has made you forget yourself. We are in a tavern drinking ale, but we must not forget God!'

Cromwell stared as he spoke, but was not angry, realising Joanne had affected the young Major. Steven immediately knew he had been remiss in his manners.

'Please forgive me, sir,' he said, placing the spoon and bread back on the table, and bowed his head.

Cromwell lowered his head and said grace, 'Dear Lord, thank you for this opportunity to eat in this tavern in the company of honest men and women, and for the fine food. Amen.' Steven echoed the last word and then both men could sample the steak pie and fresh bread served in the Three Tuns.

They enjoyed the food so much, neither spoke, apart from Cromwell enquiring whether Steven was married or betrothed. He realised he knew little of the young major's private life, despite the hours they had spent in each other's company, and this caused him to feel some regret that he did not give a thought to the other's personal circumstances. His question was prompted by the way Steven had stared at the young woman, clearly attracted by her beauty, and it was a relief to hear the major say, 'No,' to his question, as he would have been disappointed to see one of his officers look at a woman thus if that man was married or betrothed. Little else was said as they ate, and after ten minutes they had finished their meal, wiping the plate clean with the last pieces of bread.

'By my word, Steven, that was a fine steak pie!' Cromwell said, and raised his hand to his mouth to suppress a rude burp. 'Excuse me, Steven,' he said and looked around the tavern. The two guards sat patiently at their table, and neither Cromwell nor Steven had noticed, that as they were engrossed in eating, that most of the other customers had left. Then as they looked around the room, the last two finished their ale, walked over to the counter where they placed the empty cups and thanked John Wiggett. Once they had closed the door behind them the four men were the only customers remaining, and Cromwell said he had an idea.

'Sir?' Steven said.

'I have thoroughly enjoyed this excursion, Major, but if

you would indulge me, we will tarry a while longer,' he said.

'Sir?'

Cromwell stood up saying, 'Please stay here, Steven. I am going to invite the landlord and young woman to join us.' Steven replied,

'Yes, sir,' somewhat confused, but not about to object, as the prospect of sitting with the young woman was unlikely to be unpleasant. Cromwell made his way back to the counter, where John Wiggett stood. Steven could not hear what was said, but could guess as after a few moments he could see Cromwell hold out his hand to the landlord, whose face changed from a smile to a look of shock, as if an apparition had appeared. He was initially unable to speak, but eventually composed himself to shake the hand offered, followed by a deep respectful bow. Cromwell said a few more words that Steven and the guards could not hear and returned to the booth. John Wiggett stood transfixed, trying to grasp what was happening, before gathering himself and turned to enter the kitchen. For a minute there was quiet, then John and Joanne emerged, the woman ashen-faced, tidying her hair and pulling up the neckline of her shirt.

'My lord, we are honoured to have you here in the Three Tuns and be invited to your table,' John said, bowing again. Joanne copied him with a bow and a curtsey, not sure which was appropriate, adding, 'Thank you, sirs, I mean, my lords.'

'Please, do not fear, it is I who is honoured to be here in your hostelry,' Cromwell said graciously, adding, 'So we might speak freely without interruption, may I ask that we bolt the door?'

'Of course, sir,' John said, and turned to do as requested. But before he could, Cromwell said, 'Please sit,' and called out, 'Guards! Would one of you lock the door, please.' One of the guards carried out the order by bolting the door, providing them with security and privacy. John and Joanne sat next to each other, John facing Cromwell, Joanne facing

Steven, who smiled and tried to not stare. They were clearly nervous and Cromwell attempted to ease their tension by asking about their backgrounds and families, which led John to tell the story of his family owning the Three Tuns since the reign of the last Henry, and that Joanne was his niece, the daughter of his sister who married James Aker, a cooper in the village of Bow to the east of the Tower. Joanne had lived and worked at the Three Tuns these last eight years. John had been married to Margaret, but his heart was broken when she and their child died in childbirth. He could not bring himself to remarry and so Joanne became his adopted daughter and heir.

'Hopefully, she will meet a suitable young man, marry and continue our family's association with this tavern,' John explained, causing Joanne to blush in front of the young Major.

'Would you like that, Miss Joanne?' Cromwell asked, to which she replied whilst facing the table through modesty.

'Yes, sir, but meeting a suitable man is not easy inside the kitchen of a tavern.'

'How so, may I ask,' Cromwell asked.

'Sir, I mean, my lord, the men in a tavern can become coarse in their speech to a woman after two cups of ale,' Joanne said, embarrassed.

'I understand, Miss Joanne,' Cromwell said, his ire itched by the thought of drunken men speaking foul to the young woman, and he remembered why he was prejudiced against such places.

'I am sorry to hear that, miss,' Steven added, 'By my word I would...' and then he stopped realising it might be inappropriate to reveal the attraction he was feeling for Joanne.

John felt obliged to reassure the visitors that Joanne was safe. 'Sirs, rest assured, if I hear of any disrespectful words said to Joanne, the miscreant soon leaves through that door, helped on his way by me and Betsy!' John then explained who Betsy was, to Cromwell and Steven's amusement.

'Sir, my lord, may I ask why you wish to speak to us?' John said, nervously. The conversation had been pleasant,

but he still feared this might end badly for him and Joanne.
'Sir, I go to church every Sunday with Joanne, and this tavern
is respectable. I don't allow any use of our spare rooms for
whoring, and men who want to drink too much are shown
the door,' he said. Joanne blushed and lowered her head at the
mention of ladies of the night.

'Yes, your Lordship, my uncle is a good, honest man.'
Cromwell could feel their anxiety and tried to reassure them.

'Please, John Wiggett and Joanne Aker, you are not on
trial or under suspicion for any wrongdoing. We came here by
chance, as I asked Major Flain to get me away from Parliament
for an hour or two. He knew of your tavern as being of good
repute, so thought it suitable for me. Once here, I have become
interested in you as honest, hard-working people, and I want to
listen to you.'

'Listen to us, sir?' John said. 'Why would you want to
listen to us?' and he was able to smile at last. Joanne also found
she could look up and smile at the idea of the Lord Protector
listening to what her uncle and she might have to say, which
brightened the conversation for Steven.

'I know this must be a shock, but remember I am just
a man, albeit one with considerable power on this island. But
also know that I have to listen all day to men who also have
great wealth and power, whose primary aim is to hold on to
that wealth and power, when they should be serving the people,
people like you.'

John nodded his head, beginning to understand and
liking the man of manners more.

'What would you like to hear from us, sir?' John asked.

'John, I am under increasing pressure from the
aforementioned men of property and power to take action
against men and organisations who are seen as dangerous. It is
not one man, nor is it one organisation, but a multitude of men
from a collection of organisations,' Cromwell explained. John
and Joanne listened carefully, and John had an idea of whom
Cromwell spoke, but he would wait to hear more confirming

his suspicion before speaking of them.

'Which men and organisations, sir?' Joanne asked, providing the prompt for more information that John required. Steven liked the confidence to ask a question of his master, shown by the young woman opposite.

'There are men who want greater freedom to live as they choose, to have more rights to choose their representatives in Parliament, and some want a greater share of the wealth of the country,' Cromwell said, and felt the pocket of his tunic to make sure the list of names he'd been handed by Sir Charles Hadleigh was still safe.

'Well, sir. That doesn't sound unreasonable to a working man, such as myself,' John Wiggett replied. 'I have never been afforded a vote to elect an MP,' he added, and wondered if it was wise to offer such an opinion. But he was reassured by Cromwell.

'This is true, John, perhaps the ordinary man has been neglected by our Republic since 1649. Would you want to elect your church ministers, or own the land?' Cromwell asked.

'I don't know enough about religion or the different churches to choose a minister or priest, sir. It's enough for me to have somewhere to go each Sunday to commune with the Lord. The name above the door, does not matter to me. And as to the land, I do not toil the soil, but if I did, I think I might like to own a piece of it,' John replied, and there was a pause.

Cromwell liked the affable landlord even more. 'By my word, this man speaks more sense than a plethora of MPs,' he thought, and wondered how honest he would be in reply to the next question, 'Without betraying any trust, do such men meet here in the Three Tuns, John?'

It was direct and could scare the landlord from being open and helpful, but John Wiggett was not afraid. 'We have all manner of customers, sir, and I do not spy on their conversations, but it is fair to say men of all political and religious leanings have met and talked here these last twenty years. They included men who supported your cause, those who were for the King, and all manner of religious sects, that I hear speak but do not always understand,' John explained with a shrug of his shoulders, causing a smile and laugh from Cromwell.

'Aye, John. There seem to be new sects, each with their own idea of how to worship God, appearing each year. It is indeed confusing for anyone who is not a theologian,' Cromwell said, again trying to reassure his host. He decided he would not attempt to pressure the landlord into providing names and betraying confidences, but instead try to learn what these men were like.

'What kind of men are they and why do they come here, John? Speak plainly and have no fear. I give you my word, nothing you and Miss Joanne says to us here will be used to incriminate you, just as John Lilburne has argued. I seek your advice and everything you say will not be shared with others by myself and Major Flain,' Cromwell said, ready to listen.

'Well, sir,' John said, taking a deep breath. 'These men you ask of, the ones who come into the Three Tuns, they be ordinary men, and in my experience honest, hard-working men. The war seemed to change everything, with your army filled with men who wanted a better England, whether it be more equality, or greater religious freedom. You, Fairfax and the army showed ordinary men they could rise in society to become officers. And now it's over they are not willing to go back to the days of masters and subjects. I think it was called feudalism?' John paused, waiting for a response to confirm he was along the right lines, which Cromwell provided.

'Yes, John, you are correct, the war and the army did change England. None of us are subjects any longer, and Major Flain here is an example of a man from humble origin rising in society,' Cromwell said with a glance at his aide, and noticed the smile on the face of Joanne, who seemed impressed. Steven confirmed this with a polite nod. 'Why are there so many of the men in the taverns and inns here in London, John?'

Cromwell asked.

'There are different reasons for different men, sir. We see them all, and I cannot imagine how many there must be in all the hostelries of this city. I think masterless men gather in towns and cities, where they can talk, and London is the greatest of these places. In the countryside a man who questions the order of things is more easily identified, as in the villages everyone knows everyone's business,' John said, and was met with agreement by Steven.

'Aye, that be true, John,' he said, thinking of his own small hamlet about thirty miles to the north near Welwyn in Hertfordshire.

'Men seeking change are drawn to London, sir,' John continued, 'where they can find anonymity in the alleys and shadows. London seems to grow every day, sir. Just the other day, Alderman Potter who calls in weekly for a cup or two of ale, said records suggest London has grown eightfold since the days of the last King Henry a century ago, and what were once hamlets and villages an hour walk from the city walls have now been swallowed into the body of the city. Many of these new inhabitants are men such as you ask of,' John said.

Cromwell listened carefully, nodded, and said approvingly, 'Aye, I think you are accurate with your assessment, John.' He was liking this ordinary man more and wondered why he hadn't spent more time in such company.

'Then there are the poor, sir. Wretches who hide in the shadows, who may have been made homeless by landowners enclosing the land. They can find more ways to scrape a living here, doing jobs like mudlarks along the banks of the Thames. These are not bad people, sir, and may be drawn to groups who might offer more hope,' John said, and there was quiet for a moment as Cromwell considered what he had heard.

'Thank you, John Wiggett, you have been most informative. I wish I had spent more time listening to such as you,' Cromwell said, before turning to Joanne. 'And what do you say, Miss Joanne? Would you share with us your thoughts?'

'Me, sir? What would you have me say, sir?' she
replied, somewhat taken aback.

'I know you probably share your uncle's views on the
different groups of men agitating for change, but what of the
laws passed by Parliament since the regicide?' Cromwell asked.

'Regicide? Forgive me, sir, I am ill-educated and
ignorant of the meaning of that word,' Joanne replied, her face
turning red, embarrassed.

'Forgive me, Miss Joanne,' Cromwell said,
embarrassed with himself that he might make the young
woman feel uncomfortable. 'By regicide I refer to the execution
of King Charles. What do you think of the laws that have been
passed since that day in January, 1649?'

'I see,' Joanne said, realising this man, the Lord
Protector of England, was asking her, a tavern maid and cook,
what she thought about the new laws of the last five years and
how they affected women like her. 'Well, sir,' she bit her lip,
whether to speak her mind.

'Please speak freely, Miss Joanne, I value your advice
and I promise you are safe from recrimination,' Cromwell said.

'Recrimination, sir?' Joanne asked, again confused by
an unfamiliar word.

'Nothing you say will be used against you,' Cromwell
said reassuringly.

'Ah, thank you, sir. Well, if I can speak plainly, sir, I
would say women are more afraid these last five years.'

'Why so, Miss Joanne?' Cromwell asked sincerely.

'Sir, some of the laws are too cruel to women,' Joanne
said, still uncertain but the Lord Protector had promised, so
she would speak her mind. 'We have seen women who inhabit
these streets, who having fallen on hard times and must sell
their bodies to men to survive, arrested and sent as slaves
to the Americas. I know their trade is sinful, but they do it
through necessity, and the punishment seems too severe,'
Joanne said, her smile gone, replaced by a sadness that melted

Steven's heart. Cromwell was also touched by her plea, but his Puritan heart was harder than the young officer's.

'I can understand your view, Miss Joanne, showing Christian compassion, but Parliament is determined to make England a more godly nation and the law is unequivocal in dealing with this sinful practice.'

'Yes, sir, I know, but was not Mary Magdalene referred to as a 'sinful woman' in the scriptures?' Joanne asked nervously.

'Indeed, she was, but that does not mean she was a prostitute,' Cromwell replied, offering the interpretation popular amongst Protestant churches since Luther, challenging the traditional Catholic interpretation that one of Jesus' closest friends was a repentant fallen woman. But he was not interested in theological interpretation of the Bible at this moment. 'What else troubles you about the new laws, Miss Joanne?' he asked.

'Sir, the laws against fornication and adultery are also cruel to women,' Joanne said.

'Why so, men and women can both be found guilty of such immoral behaviour,' Cromwell replied.

'Yes, sir, but in practice it seems only women are found guilty and punished by male juries and judges,' Joanne retorted and continued, 'and the women found guilty are often young and simply made a bad choice in allowing themselves to be seduced by the charms of an older married man. A young woman may have been ignorant of her lover being married, or may have been lied to by him saying he was unmarried. Invariably her guilt is manifested by the illegitimate child growing in her womb, and her only defence is to claim she was raped, but her honesty and love prevents her making such a claim. Should such a young woman be hanged?' Joanne asked, causing Cromwell to think, and with this argument he had more sympathy.

'I think you make a strong advocate for these women, Miss Joanne. Do you think such men lying about their status is commonplace?' he asked.

'Sir, I cannot speak for all of the country, nor all of London, but from my experience here in the Three Tuns, I know men regularly tell lies motivated by lust,' Joanne said, 'but I am accustomed to their advances when my uncle is not near.'

Both Cromwell and Steven bristled at the thought of dishonest men making lustful advances to this good, honest young woman, but realised it was likely to be an occupational hazard in such a place as the Three Tuns.

'I regret to hear this, Miss Joanne,' Cromwell said, adding, 'though I am sure your uncle here will always defend you against such men.'

'Aye, sir, Betsy and I are here for my niece, and all my regulars know it, but sometimes strangers get too familiar, particularly I am sorry to say, so-called gentlemen with money and a sense of entitlement.'

Cromwell nodded, 'I know of such men, John. I hope there are fewer of them after the defeat of the Royalists by our more godly army.'

'Aye, sir, I think the war did remove a good number of such men, but sadly they seem to have been replaced by others, as generations replace those who went before them,' John said philosophically. 'I think it comes with wealth and power, John,' Cromwell replied, and the two older men found themselves nodding in agreement.

Eventually, the meeting in the Three Tuns came to an end and it was time to make their way back to Westminster. Cromwell thanked John Wiggett and Joanne Aker for their time and their honesty. He could not guarantee changes but said he valued and would remember everything they had discussed. Goodbyes were said, and John finished by saying, 'We cannot tell anyone of this meeting, no one will believe us and we're likely to end up in Bedlam!' All four were able to share some laughter, and Cromwell, Steven and the two guards left. Steven was the last to leave through the main door, and as he did so he looked back at Joanne, who was looking directly at him. Steven took a moment to smile and gave a respectful bow, before joining the other three and they made their way through the grey slush-covered street leading to Whitehall.

December 1653

Christmas had passed uneventfully, which was how many of the country's masters wished it to be, some fearing agitators would seize upon the reduced festivities to spread their poison and demands for political and religious reform. Oliver Cromwell's family were no longer small children, the youngest, Frances and Mary, being fifteen and sixteen years of age. Therefore, the demand for festivities was not apparent in their family, but over the twelve days that traditionally marked the period as a time of joyous celebration, he found himself thinking about the past. He also thought about the boy who would have been his and Elizabeth's next youngest, James. 'Poor James, you did not even see your first birthday, dying in 1632, the year of your birth,' he thought, as he looked out over the terrace at Hampton Court. 'You would be twenty-one years if you had not been taken so young.' Then his thoughts returned to Christmas celebrations and how they were disapproved of by Puritan Parliament. 'Drunkenness and debauchery are sinful but is it so bad for ordinary folk to seek pleasure to puncture the tedium of daily toil?' he thought. He found himself sinking into melancholy, wondering if this title of Lord Protector was too heavy a burden. 'Was making England a more godly country too great a task for a man, albeit one with almost absolute power? Do we go too far with these laws dictating how men and women should behave and worship?' Such thoughts seemed to be recurring on a regular basis as he heard more about the prosecution of people for breaching the morality laws of the last five years. His conversations with Major Flain enlightened him of the mood in the army, and they were concerning. The visit to the Three Tuns tavern near Charing Cross was also occupying his thoughts when he found himself considering these matters, and the words of two ordinary folk like John Wiggett and Joanne Aker were more prominent than the ramblings of MPs like Sir

Charles Hadleigh, James Banstead and Jonathan Marlow.

The afternoon passed and evening set in as the sun disappeared to the west. At supper he realised an episode might be coming as he found his appetite wane, replaced by nausea. His brow became more furrowed, his face contorted by the discomfort. Elizabeth had seen it before and reached over to hold his hand, wanting to help.

'Shall I prepare your bed, husband?' she asked, by which she meant the bed would have extra clean sheets to hand, as well as a spare nightshirt, the likelihood being he would be in need of them before the morning. One of the many luxuries of his status and their new home being a palace built by Cardinal Wolsley and gifted to King Henry, was a surfeit of bedrooms. When one of his episodes occurred, he was most comfortable alone in one of the simple smaller bedrooms, with a jug of water and warm fire.

'Dear Elizabeth, why should you share in the suffering of this curse?' he said to himself as she went to prepare the room.

The melancholy of the afternoon continued as he lay in bed waiting for sleep to provide some relief from the fever and chills which, as expected, arrived following the nausea during supper. He was still alert and his thoughts from the afternoon continued to dominate his mind, but he eventually fell asleep.

'Men demanding land, spouting sedition and heresy,' Sir Charles Hadleigh whispered in his ear. 'They will demand your family's land in Cambridgeshire, Lord Protector. Lollards from centuries ago, they have never gone away. They became Diggers, then Levellers, and now Quakers, turning the world and the natural order on its head,' Hadleigh kept pursuing him, like the leader of a pack of wolves. 'What are you going to do, Lord Protector?' Hadleigh and his cronies had him cornered, demanding he act, 'the boil has to be lanced, Lord Protector!' He squirmed to get free of the pack but there seemed to be no escape as they closed in on him, snarling, baring long canine teeth and saliva. The pack of wolves disappeared, replaced by John Wiggett and his niece, the innocent Joanne. 'John Wiggett,' he said, 'some say you are suggesting sedition and heresy, if you say all men should vote for MPs and church ministers.' 'Yes, sir, I must be guilty if that be what makes a man seditious or heretic. I am sorry, sir,' John Wiggett replied. 'The law, John Wiggett, it's the law!' he said, the simple statement being all the explanation that was necessary. 'Therefore, John Wiggett, you must hang, it's the law!' 'Yes, sir,' the noble tavern landlord replied. 'You, Joanne Aker, what say you?' he asked. 'These laws punish women unfairly, sir.' 'How so, Joanne?' 'Your laws send fallen women as slaves to the Americas. Others are hanged for the mistake of being intimate with a married man. Men can humiliate their wives with a scold's bridle.' 'Joanne, you say, "Your laws," but these are our laws, the laws passed by Parliament for the country.' 'No, sir!' Joanne retorted, raising her voice and he was shocked. 'These laws are YOUR laws, passed by men for the benefit of men. How do they serve women, sir?' Her anger abated and she hung her head, but he could see a tear appear in the corner of her eye.

He woke from the dream, which was still vivid in his mind. The fever had passed, but as usual the sheets of his bed and nightshirt were damp, so he took a couple of minutes to haul himself up and out of the bed, replacing those items with the dry ones Elizabeth had laid on the table to the side of the room. Across the room the fire had burnt down but could be revived, so he added three logs and used the poker to stoke it back to life. He got back into bed, watching the flames rise and thought about his dreams, which seemed to frequently occur in his sleep during an episode when a fever had hold of him.

'Is this God's way of forcing me to reflect on what we have done?' he muttered to himself. 'MPs and Parliament. The morality laws. Have we gone too far? Dissenters and ordinary hard-working folk like John Wiggett and Joanne Aker,' he said quietly to himself, 'have we failed to listen to them?'

Staring at the fire, which could be relied on to have

125

a soporific effect, his last thought before falling asleep was Joanne's anger and sadness, and the tear in her eye.

***

William Fogg's home and business was located on Halliers Lane, in the shadow of the city wall that followed the River Froome, which flowed east to west, before turning south to join the River Avon. The building had stood for almost a century, built by his great-grandfather at the beginning of Gloriana's reign. His father, James, had carried on the family business and happily handed it over to William when he was in his fiftieth year. James and his wife, Margaret, were able to move into a small cottage the other side of the Froome, from where they were close enough to help with the business if required. Similarly, William and Elizabeth's four children could reach their grandparents cottage in six minutes if they ran without stopping to catch their breath, a challenge each one quickly mastered.

'Safe journey, husband,' Elizabeth said as William picked up the reins.

'Thank you, my love. Stay warm and dry,' he replied as he looked up at the sky. Dark clouds were moving in from the west, as they always did sweeping in from the Atlantic and up the Severn Estuary. 'I will be just a few days,' he added, and shook the reins. 'Get on, Jessie. You too, Mabel,' and with that familiar tone the two horses pulled the cart into motion.

It was just a short trip to Bath, just twelve miles, and then another twenty-eight to Swindon, requiring a night in the Wiltshire town. Jessie and Mabel pulled William's cart southwards through the busy roads of Bristol, crossing the bridge over the Avon and turning south east along the Bath Road. The noise and smells of the city were soon left behind, and William was left to his thoughts as he relaxed his grip on the reins, allowing Jessie and Mabel to proceed at their own pace. Despite the threat of inclement weather, he enjoyed these hours on the road, alone to reflect on his pleasures. He had not seen Susan for some weeks and missed the warmth of her body and her tender kisses, which led him the previous day to read the two letters she had written, the second just weeks after they made love in August. Disappointingly, there was no opportunity to repeat the act when he was able to call in to Honiton in September; just a few moments alone together when she handed him the folded parchment. Having read both letters many times in the following months, riding out of Bristol he found himself comparing her to the other women with whom he had been intimate. 'She is innocent in the ways of satisfying a man,' he thought to himself, 'which is to be expected of a maid.' He smiled. 'Do not be greedy, William, it is against reason to expect a young woman, never touched by a man, to be knowing of the carnal arts,' and his thoughts moved from Susan to other women he knew in surrounding counties and towns, and he could not resist the desire to be satisfied by a woman more skilled in pleasing a man. Paula Holt in Swindon was such a woman, who he had not visited for almost a year. A widow of forty years of age with five children, she was always pleased to see him, grateful for his company and a shilling or two, and she was well aware of how to please a man beyond simply opening her legs. 'If Susan had Paula's skills, she would be worthy of the harem of the Sultan of the Turks,' William said aloud with no one to hear, and Jessie's ears pricked up as if she was listening to him. So, he continued, 'Well, I will see my beautiful girl again soon enough, Jessie, and perhaps with time I can teach her. In the meantime, I think we should make our way to Bath and then Swindon, where I hope mistress Holt can accommodate me for an evening.' With his mind filled with images of Susan and Paula, the ache in William's loins persuaded him a stop-over in Swindon was required.

In the afternoon, several hours after her husband's departure, the dark clouds that had gathered over Bristol finally decided to deposit their load and heavy rain poured down on the city and surrounding countryside. It was torrential and visibility was hampered as it bounced off tiled roofs and streams appeared along the roads, streets and alleyways.

People quickly took shelter indoors and the thoroughfares emptied. Elizabeth looked out of the window at the deserted streets and up at the darkened skies.

'There does not appear to be any wind, Margaret, so I think this downpour will be with us for the rest of the day,' she said to her eldest child, who helped her in the shop.

'Shall we remain open, mother?' Margaret asked.

'I think it would not profit us to remain open, Margaret, as only inmates escaped from Bedlam in London would be out in this weather,' her mother replied. 'Our time can be spent more usefully with other tasks, daughter.'

'Yes, mother?' Margaret asked.

'I have been intending to clean the shop thoroughly for some time, my dear. Perhaps this afternoon is opportune,' and as she spoke Elizabeth moved over to the door, securing it with the main bolt.

'Yes, mother,' Margaret repeated, this time without curiosity, which was replaced by some disappointment at the prospect of the task ahead.

Within fifteen minutes mother and daughter were ready to begin, wearing aprons and armed with scrubbing brushes, various cloths, and a bucket. Into each bucket Elizabeth poured hot water heated from the open fire, to which was added soap and a strong apple vinegar, Elizabeth's own recipe for cleaning, producing an unpleasant aroma that filled Margaret's senses. But the girl knew there was little point in protesting, rather she steeled herself to the task, looking forward to its completion.

'Margaret, would you clean the shop, please. Start with the shelves and counter, then scrub the floor. There is plenty of hot water in the hearth, so use it generously, adding more soap and vinegar as needed. I will work on the storeroom, where the rolls of cloth may be too heavy for you.'

'Yes, mother,' she repeated, again, this time with a resigned tone.

Elizabeth left Margaret to get on with her task and entered the storeroom at the back of the shop, where shelves lined the walls, stacked with dozens of rolls of cloth. She and William had them arranged by fabric and colour, woollen cloth being the greatest in number, with smaller numbers of rolls of fine linen, lace from the Netherlands, cotton and silk from the Orient. These exotic materials being rare were accordingly more expensive. In the middle of the room was a large table, covered in loose cuttings, some tidied into piles of similar size and cloth, other pieces lay where they were cut and left. An old jug contained an assortment of scissors and sharp knives, and some of these were spread across the table.

'Right, where shall I start?' Elizabeth said to herself and looked around the storeroom.

She set herself to the table, placing all scissors and knives in the large jug, then gathering the cuttings into tidy piles. Some fine lace caught her eye, and she paused for a moment to hold it against her face. Her mind wandered back to when she was a maid, barely eighteen years of age, and how William, just a few years older, would bring her gifts of fine materials like this piece of lace. Combined with his natural charm, she was smitten by his beautiful gifts, which he could procure from his father's storeroom, the very space in which she stood. They courted for almost a year and wed when she was still eighteen and William twenty-one. He was devoted to her, and four healthy children were born by her twenty-fifth birthday. Then she was taken ill, and her monthly bleeding became heavier, leaving her tired and weak. Physicians attended to her, and after examination, suggested she may not be able to have more children, but with care she could live a good life. Elizabeth, William, and their families were relieved she would survive, but for her this initial relief was followed by a feeling of disappointment, even failure. Two more pregnancies both resulted in miscarriages and further illness requiring convalescence. William was concerned for her well-being, and she realised as time passed their marriage had changed. Nights of intimacy faded away, and by the time she was thirty years of age, seemed to have disappeared from their lives. He remained a good husband and father, but he was no longer her lover. In truth, she did not miss it at the time as she was busy raising their four healthy children, for whom she was grateful, as well as helping in the shop, particularly when he was away on the road, and she was often tired. But every now and then, like this moment alone in the storeroom, she found time to reflect on the last seventeen years and how she missed the feeling of her husband's flesh pressed firmly against her body. Stood there in the storeroom she felt melancholy, but then the reality of life and her role brought her back to the present.

'Stop dwelling on what might be missing from your life, woman, you are most fortunate to have a good husband, four healthy children and a secure home,' she said to herself. 'Banish self-pity and get on with your work.'

She looked around the storeroom at the piles of cloth stacked on shelves that lined the walls. Some were neatly piled, others needed removing from the shelves, folding and returning. William had always insisted he did this task for the higher shelves, which were beyond her reach, so in the past they worked as a team, she tidying the lower shelves, while he did the higher ones.

'Perhaps I could manage those higher shelves as well, if I stand on the chair.' She thought to herself. 'Margaret!' she called through to the shop.

'Yes, mother?' the girl said, appearing in the doorway between the shop and storeroom.

'Would you kindly bring John down to assist me,' Elizabeth said, already standing on the chair, having moved it from the table to the shelves. Minutes later her fifteen-year-old son was alongside her, placing the rolls of material onto the large table as she passed them down from the top shelves.

'Thank you, John. We will get them all down onto the table, where I can tidy them and dust the shelves. Then you can return when I call to help me return them.'

'Yes, mother,' the boy replied.

Mother and son set to the task handling the rolls with care, starting with the woollen cloths, cotton, linen, lace, and even some small rolls of exotic silk.

'Take care to not drop these, John,' his mother urged, 'they come from the Orient, and cost your father a small fortune. Although whether they were worth it, I do not know, as we sell so little of it, particularly with a Puritan Parliament.'

As she said these last words, Elizabeth was looking down at the boy, so she did not notice the wooden spool of a roll of silk, around which the fine material was wound, knocked against the wall, which was panelled with wood. Having passed the valuable roll to John, she turned back to gather the next roll to see a small piece of the wooden panels had opened outwards, which on closer inspection was found to be a door. She paused, surprised, and opened it to reveal a space, in which sat a small stack of documents.

'Mother, is something wrong, are you unwell?' John asked, concerned for the pause and quiet with his mother stood on the chair, staring at the wall.

'Yes, all is well, my darling. I was just thinking,' she said, and stepped down. 'John, I thank you for your assistance, but now you can leave me to tidy these rolls, and I will call you when I need you to help me to place them back.'

'Thank you, mother,' he replied, not needing further urging and returned to the living room upstairs to watch the rain continuing to fall.

Elizabeth moved the chair back to the table and looked up to the shelf where the small panel was hidden from sight. 'It must be a secret place, where William keeps important documents. But why has he not shared this with me?' she thought. 'What does he need to hide from me, his wife?'

For a few minutes Elizabeth did nothing as she pondered the mystery of the panel in the wall. 'Should I look inside at the documents? What would he wish to keep secret from me?' she thought, and felt uneasy in herself, almost nauseous. 'If I look inside, would this make me a distrustful wife? He must have good reasons to keep these things from me.' Her curiosity turned to guilt, freezing her for a few moments, uncertain of what to do. She looked around to see if any of the children were present, but none were nearby or watching. She could hear Margaret scrubbing the floor in the shop, and she realised that even if they were watching, they could not see the panel due to its position at the back of the shelf. Gathering her thoughts, her curiosity got the better of her guilt, so she moved the chair back to the shelf and stepped up onto it. The little panel door was still open, and she reached in to carefully lift the documents out and place them on the empty shelf. There were too many to read through them there, but she could see the top one was entitled, *Last Will and Testament, James Fogg.* 'William has a copy of his father's will,' she thought. The next document read, *Title Deeds to the Property of 6 Halliers Lane, Bristol, in the County of Gloucestershire.* 'And the deeds to this building,' she thought, and suddenly the guilt of a few minutes earlier prevailed over her curiosity, so she gathered the documents together, placed them back into the space in the wall and gently closed the panel.

Returning to the table, Elizabeth continued with what she reminded herself she should be doing as a good wife, tidying the rolls of material before they could be returned to their respective shelves. When this task was completed, she called for John, who dutifully returned to the storeroom to assist her, passing the rolls up to her for the higher shelves. Soon enough, the task was completed, and she thanked both Margaret and John for their assistance, promising Margaret a piece of lace to make a nice neckerchief. However, on returning the few rolls of silk she left a space clear on the shelf in front of the panel.

The afternoon turned into evening, Elizabeth and the four children ate supper, and after they had gone to bed, she found herself in one of the large chairs by the fire, alone with her thoughts. There was no point in retiring to her bed, her mind was churning over the thoughts ignited by her discovery in the storeroom. 'Curiosity, guilt, hidden secrets, am I being a good wife, was William being deceitful?' She picked up two more logs, carefully placing them on to the fire, which at this late hour, was something she would not normally do, instead letting the fire burn down to mere embers and its heat dissipating. The flames wrapped themselves around the new sacrifice and in return radiated more heat, which would last at least another thirty minutes. For a minute, she sat looking into the flames enveloping the logs, then taking a solitary candle held firm on its pricket, she descended the stairs to the shop and storeroom.

She moved the chair over to the shelves where the exotic cloths and materials were stacked, stepped up onto the chair with care, holding the candlestick and placing it on the top shelf, which thankfully had enough space around and above to avoid burning anything. She was not sure how much force was required, so pressed the panel gently and it remained closed. Using the palm of her hand, she gave the panel a firm tap and as her hand drew back it opened. There was no hesitation, her mind was set, she gathered the documents and placed them on the chair, collected the candlestick and stepped down. Moving the chair back to the table, she returned to the living room with the candlestick in one hand, the documents gripped firmly in the other.

Settled in the large chair in front of the fire, which continued to burn, she sat for a minute simply staring at the small pile of documents. Having reached the point in her subterfuge when she would examine each of the documents her husband had hidden from her, the guilt returned. 'I could return them to the panel now, without reading them,' she thought, 'William does not need to know I discovered this place of secrecy.' Her father-in-law's will still sat at the top of the pile, and she lifted the two pages of that documents to reveal the Title of Deeds to the house. 'But what other documents would he want to keep from me?' she thought, and from somewhere in her mind emerged suspicion. She did not

133

want to think what dark secrets might emerge from the words on the pages on her lap, but she felt an intuitive sense of dread that something would be revealed. So it was that Elizabeth looked further into what her husband might have to hide. She was alone in the room and could take her time, slowly turning each page, and about halfway through the pile of contracts and bills of sale, she found what she had feared.

Dearest William

June 1653, Honiton

> *Thank you for your letter, which I cherish and keep close to me at all times.*

Elizabeth's heart stopped for a moment and she froze, reading the first line again, followed by the rest of the letter, the words assaulting her mind, heart and emotions.

> *true love, feelings and emotions changing me...nor desire to go back...I want you more and more each day...Like you, I long to embrace you, kiss your lips, and much more my love...If we cannot be man and wife here, I would go with you to the New World...our desires cannot be denied. With much love and longing until we next meet...Susan*

'Susan? Honiton?' she said to herself quietly. Her emotions were tearing her apart, as one moment she felt distraught, betrayed, then anger. Then she remembered, 'Jonathan Bounty is one of his favoured customers in that town, and he has mentioned the eldest daughter, Susan...' she thought. 'No wonder he enjoyed visiting that town, "wonderful hospitality," he said.' Pages of documents that had laid on top of the letter fell to the floor as tears streamed down her cheeks, and she wept in a way she had not since her last miscarriage seven years earlier. She held the letter with both hands, reading it again, an initial disbelief turning to inquisitiveness, searching for any detail she might have missed on first reading. 'Are there more,' she wondered, and placed the letter on the floor with the documents that had fallen from her lap. The same handwriting.

My darling William

August 1653, Honiton

    It is just two weeks since you were here, and I miss
you so much my love... my body aches to be in your arms,
connected as one entity, flesh to flesh...

Elizabeth felt sick, this second letter going further
in its description, and for a moment she thought it might be
describing a young woman's fantasy, what she desired, but then
came the words confirming it was not a young girl's dream.

    William I was a maid until this month, something I
thought would last until my wedding night, but I am pleased
and grateful that I gave my honour to you, and I will live with
the consequences, whatever they may be...

She sat back in the chair, her tears ceased, replaced by
a rage moving through her body. 'Damn you, Susan Bounty.
Your desire and pleasure would ruin my family,' she whispered
staring into the fire. Her anger with the girl left her feeling
drained and as the fire burned down, she leaned forward to
gather the documents from the floor. 'Husband,' she thought,
'did I deserve this?' and her thoughts turned from the girl to
him. 'Have I failed you as a wife?' and her emotions changed
again, anger turning to more tears. There was no need to
return the documents to their home in the wooden panels of
the storeroom, so she took them to her room, placing them
carefully under the bed. The bed in which she and William
used to be intimate in the way the girl described in her letters.

    In bed, Elizabeth lay awake, emotionally drained and
alone. Her thoughts about the girl were settled and she resolved
to make her pay dearly. But her feelings towards her husband
differed. He had betrayed their vows and the trust she placed
in him, wronging her most cruelly, and yet she found herself
wondering if it was not entirely his fault. She remembered
the whispered conversations of women in the marketplace, of
sterile marriages in which men looked elsewhere for the carnal
warmth no longer provided by their wives. 'Is this what we
have become, husband?' she thought. 'Is this what has driven
you to look elsewhere for satisfaction of your needs?' A tear

moved down her cheek as misplaced guilt grew in her mind, mitigation for William's sin. Sleep did not come easily to her relief and, as she waited, she resolved to do something the next day about the girl, Susan Bounty. What she should do, or could do, about William was less certain.

Elizabeth was awake early, the sun yet to rise in the east, feeling as if she had not slept. There was no need to return the documents to the space behind the wall panel until later, as William would not arrive home before late afternoon when the sun was setting. Therefore, she took care to hide the documents within her bedsheets and blankets, minus the two letters from the girl. Once the children were awake and fed breakfast, she told Margaret to take care of them as she had an errand in town.

Just a walk of ten minutes from the shop, Elizabeth was stood outside Bristol's Guildhall, its great wooden doors lined by carvings of men practising their crafts and trades. Stonemasons, carpenters, ironmongers, draughtsmen, and there was a clothier, representing the merchants to which her husband owed his livelihood. For a moment she stood staring at the sculptures, thinking about how the action she was about to take might affect her family, and whether it would survive. However, she was decided to proceed and walked through the doorway past two guards, where she was met by an officer of the city council.

'Good day, madam. Do you have business here today?' he asked, curious why an unattended woman should be at a place that represented the merchants, crafts and trades of men.

'Good day to you, sir. I do not have business with any of the different guilds of this place, but I wish to speak to the commissioner who represents the will of Parliament and the Commonwealth,' Elizabeth replied, hoping the mention of those higher institutions would persuade the council officer to allow her entry. He looked at the woman stood before him, clearly respectable from her dress.

'What is it you would speak of to the commissioner,

madam?' he asked.

'Sir, it is of a personal and delicate matter, but pertains to breaches of the laws passed by Parliament to make England more godly. Therefore, I would ask to speak directly to the commissioner, lest knowledge of infringements should be compromised.'

She spoke articulately, persuading the officer he had better see if the commissioner could listen to her case. 'Very well, madam, please sit on the bench and I will send word of your request,' he said gesturing to a long bench along the wall to the left of the doors.

'Thank you, sir,' Elizabeth replied and sat waiting.

A boy was beckoned from the shadows of the entrance and took a written note into the main hall, disappearing through crowds of men going about the business of their chosen guild. The boy was gone for ten minutes, leaving Elizabeth to sit and wait, but then returned and spoke to the council officer.

'Madam, the commissioner can receive you now. This boy will take you to the commissioner's quarters.'

'Thank you, sir,' Elizabeth said, stood up and followed the boy into the main hall and through the throng. As the boy weaved his way between different groups, members of each group politely stepped back to allow Elizabeth more space so she did not have to brush against them, recognising the discomfort a solitary woman might feel in the male-dominated commercial environment of the Guildhall. At the far end of the hall was a door in one corner with a wooden bench to the side.

'Please wait here, missus,' the lad said. He was no older than her youngest, possibly eleven years of age, and as she sat down, he seemed to go through the doorway barely opening the door, squeezing through the narrowest space and closing it behind him. Again, Elizabeth was left to wait, her nerves building as she thought about how she would tell the commissioner of the sin and crime of a young woman in Honiton. A few minutes passed as the other side of the door the commissioner concluded a piece of business regarding drunkenness and blasphemy. Then the boy repeated the feat of managing to exit the room with only the smallest of openings of the door.

'The commissioner will see you now, missus, if you would come through,' he said.

Inside the room a man sat at a long table with another man to his left. They were both dressed in the plain black clothes of Puritans, a modest piece of white lace lining the collars of their tunics. In front of the smaller man to the side were piles of documents and a selection of quills and ink wells. The larger man sat with nothing directly in front of him as his forearms rested on the table with his hands entwined as if he was about to pray. It was he who spoke, the smaller man waiting with quill and paper, ready to record any necessary details as requested.

'I am Godswill Brown, madam, Parliament's commissioner for the south-west of England. Please be seated and tell me of what you think I should be made aware,' he said gesturing towards the solitary chair the other side of the table. The chair was set back six feet so the person who sat on it would feel isolated, as they might if on trial, and they could not see what might be recorded by the commissioner's scribe.

'Thank you, sir,' Elizabeth replied nervously, accepting his invitation.

Godswill Brown stared at the woman sat ten feet away, saying nothing for a few moments as he considered her demeanour and appearance. In his role as commissioner he had met women of all backgrounds, social class and occupations. 'This one seems respectable enough; she is certainly dressed modestly. Well, let's find out what her complaint might be,' he thought.

'Good day, madam. What is it you wish to bring to my attention?' he said coldly, staring directly at the woman, looking for any signs of deceit. So it was that Elizabeth Fogg was able to explain to Parliament's commissioner for the south-west of England how she and her family had been wronged by a young woman's desires, fornication and adultery.

He listened intently to every detail, his cold stare only leaving the plaintiff's eyes when she passed him the evidence. Showing no emotion, Godswill Brown read both letters twice. He handed them to his aide and looked up at Elizabeth.

'We will keep these letters as evidence that may be required in a court of law,' he said.

'Yes, sir.'

'Mrs Fogg, this is a most grievous breach of the laws of England and God. Leave this matter with me for further investigation,' was all he said, followed by a loud call, 'Boy!'

The same small boy appeared from behind and stood beside Elizabeth.

'Escort Mrs Fogg to the entrance, Arthur, and then report back to me, as I may have some correspondence for you to deliver,' he said to the boy, then turned to Elizabeth, 'Thank you, Mrs Fogg.'

Elizabeth stood up without further word, followed Arthur out of the room and within minutes was outside on the streets of Bristol making her way home to her family.

January 1654

Joanne Aker was clearing tables of the detritus left by groups of men, who had eaten dinner without the civilising influence of women upon their table manners. Pieces of bread, pastry and the contents of various pies littered the tables and the floor. 'Sometimes I wonder if the men who eat here transfer less from plate to mouth, than they do to the table and floor,' she said to herself, as she bent down with a brush to gather the offending morsels into a neat pile. She wore an apron, her sleeves were rolled up for the task of cleaning, and her long fair hair was tied back to prevent it from falling into food that may have fallen from a customer's mouth as he probably attempted to sup ale whilst eating. Her uncle was tending to one of the barrels perched in a recess in the wall that separated the kitchen from the main room of the tavern where men could eat and drink.

'Aye, Joanne, they would not be welcome at the table of a fine lady, but here they feel unleashed from the bridle of politeness,' he said.

'I suppose I do not qualify as a lady?'

'Do not be offended, niece. See it as a compliment that they feel comfortable in your company,' John Wiggett said in a light-hearted tone. He understood her disquiet, and loss of patience, when constantly clearing up after men who showed her less respect than they might because of her occupation.

'Dear God, they eat like pigs!' she said as she tried to gather one particularly recalcitrant mass of ale-soaked pie and bread that would not move.

'Joanne, this is true of men when they have been supping ale, and it is our misfortune to suffer their coarseness. But it provides us with a home and a living.'

'I know, uncle, I know,' she replied, having heard those words many times.

Looking down at the floor and concentrating on her

task, she did not notice a man with a familiar face enter through the main door, but her uncle did.

'Good morning, Major. What brings you to the Three Tuns on this chilly winter morning?'

Joanne froze on hearing the word, 'Major', as she could think of only one man of that rank who her uncle might know. Steven Flain had filled her thoughts for many hours since the unexpected visit of the Lord Protector a couple of months ago, particularly when considering if all men were of the nature of their customers after four or five cups of ale. She had decided she was being delusional thinking he, a Major, might consider her, a tavern maid, a suitable match. However, vaulting ambition remained, thoughts of him brightening her day during her daily toil. Now, that word, 'Major,' meant he had returned, but instead of joy, she was struck by horror as she thought of how he would see her, on her hands and knees, cleaning.

'Good morning, Mr Wiggett, I was passing and thought I would call in to bid you and Miss Joanne good health,' Steven said smiling.

'Joanne, it's Major Flain,' her uncle said, as if she was unaware of his presence. 'Come girl, stand up and show our visitor both manners and a welcome.

'Oh, Major Flain, please forgive me,' Joanne said raising her head whilst still on all fours, then stood up. There was no face she would rather see, but she was embarrassed by her appearance, as strands of hair escaped their tie and fell across her face. For a moment she stood facing Steven, no words were spoken, and she could not know the sight of her in a state of toil enhanced his admiration.

'Miss Joanne, I apologise for interrupting you from your labours. Perhaps I should have asked before calling.'

She gathered the miscreant strands and placed them back with the rest of her hair, trying to hide the nervousness caused by her visitor. 'My only regret is if I had known of your visit, I would have completed my cleaning duties earlier, Major.'

John Wiggett broke the awkwardness of the moment.

'Please sit down, Major Flain, it is a pleasure for us to see you. Have a cup of ale and tell us of the Lord Protector and matters of the outside world of which we are ignorant.'

'Thank you, sir,' Steven replied and joined John at a table.

'Joanne, bring three cups of ale, and join us,' John said.

Pleasantries were exchanged and after ten minutes Steven felt he should get to the point of his visit.

'Sir, miss, I have to confess I did not call in by accident. I walked to Charing Cross with a specific purpose this morning.'

'What is it, Major? I hope nothing is amiss or ails you?' John said, concerned, which was shared by Joanne, though she remained quiet.

'Well, sir, it is this,' he replied, then paused, searching for the words he had rehearsed but now escaped him. 'Sir, miss, I have thought of you both since the impromptu visit with the Lord Protector two months ago. Both he and I were impressed with our conversations that day, and he mentions you frequently.' Then he paused again.

'Yes, Major. We are honoured to hear that the most important man in England should be impressed by folk as lowly as ourselves,' John said, sensing that was not the purpose of Steven's visit. 'Is there something else you wish to say, Major?'

'Yes, sir.' Steven was surprised that he was finding it difficult to express himself. 'I have thought of you both with respect and admiration, but I have also become aware of an interest to learn more about you, with a view to becoming a friend and possibly more, if circumstances allow.'

'Yes, Major?' John asked, as Joanne looked on hoping.

'I would most respectfully ask if I may, with the consent of you both, walk with Joanne one morning or afternoon?' he said, looking at John and then Joanne, with a feeling of awkward embarrassment, as if he was a young boy rather than an army major.

Both John and Joanne were taken aback by the request, the former smiling before replying, 'Well, that is a welcome surprise, Major Flain, and as her uncle, I see no objection to such a polite request from a gentleman as yourself. But what does the young lady in question say?' he asked turning to Joanne.

Joanne was surprised, but if she was to be honest, she would admit it was a question she had aspired to hear those last two months. 'Am I hearing correctly?' she thought, and a wide smile appeared across her face.

'Sir, I am flattered to be asked to walk with a gentleman like yourself. It is not the usual approach I receive from men,' she said, alluding to the customers who feel amorous after drinking ale. 'I think it would be most pleasant to spend time in your company one morning or afternoon, if my uncle can spare me for an hour from my duties?'

'By my word, I am sure I can survive without you here for a couple of hours in a morning, Joanne,' John said with a smile, delighted that his niece might enjoy a break from work with a man like Major Flain, of whom he thought highly after the visit in November.

The relief for both Joanne and Steven was in equal measure and it was agreed they could walk together after church on the next Sunday, just three days hence. Joanne did not have much to say, she just smiled in a slight state of shock. Steven left the Three Tuns pleased that he had gathered the courage to make his approach, satisfying the question that had been in his thoughts for almost two months; could Joanne Aker find him as pleasing to her eye as she was to his?

Sunday morning finally arrived and as usual John and his niece attended a morning service at St Martin-in-the-Fields, the ancient church dating back to the first English Christians that had been extended fifty years earlier by the Scottish king. As they walked the short distance back to the Three Tuns, Joanne seemed impatient and in a hurry.

'You seem in great haste, niece. Have you something that requires your urgent attention?' John asked, aware that Major Flain was due to call, but unable to resist some teasing.

'Yes, uncle. Have you forgotten I have an appointment

this day?'

'An appointment? What appointment?'

'Uncle!' she exclaimed, 'you know Major Flain is taking me out walking!' Joanne sounded indignant that John could have forgotten.

'Ah, Major Flain. Of course, how could I forget?' and he decided to end any ruse, realising this was an important matter to the young woman. 'Why should she not look forward to and enjoy an hour or two with the young officer,' he thought. 'God knows she works hard enough and has so little pleasure,' and as he looked at her, as they marched with purpose back to the tavern, he felt the fondness and pride a man would have for his daughter.

Within thirty minutes Joanne was sitting waiting nervously, but she need not have worried as Steven had no intention of being late and, like her, had looked forward to his visit since Thursday. He was not disappointed when he saw her sitting modestly in her best Sunday clothes, warm winter coat, boots, and a headscarf that hid all but two strands of golden hair.

'Good day to you, Miss Joanne.'

'Good day to you, Major Flain.'

For a moment neither knew what to say next, waiting for the other to speak, until the quiet was broken by John.

'Well, if you are going to stand there in silence, I will leave you to meditate. I have work to do,' and he turned to attend to his tasks behind the bar, adding with a smile, 'perhaps you would prefer to sit at a table and stare at each other.'

'Ah, thank you, sir. You are right, we should be on our way. Shall we go, Miss Joanne?'

'Yes, Major, I think we should,' Joanne replied, and the couple made their way from the Three Tuns in the direction of the river.

'Where should we walk, Major?' Joanne asked, curious but not worried, as an hour or two in the company of this man was as pleasant a pastime as she could imagine.

'Well, I thought it might be both pleasant and interesting

to cross the river, walk along the south bank, crossing over the bridge, then returning along the Strand. If that is to your liking?'

Joanne did not mind where they went, although crossing the river in January was not something she would normally countenance.

'That sounds perfect, Major,' she replied with a warm smile that reassured Steven.

'It may be cold in the boat crossing the river, Joanne. I am glad to see you are wearing a winter coat and headscarf.'

Within five minutes they were down by the Thames at a small jetty known as Charing Cross Steps. Moored on either side were five or six boats with their oars pulled in. At the land end of the jetty on firm ground a brazier burned surrounded by half a dozen men trying to keep warm. As the couple approached the men looked up, one of them calling, 'Good day to you, Major!'

'Good day to you, Paul. Is it possible to employ a wherryman to get us safely to the other side of the river?' Steven asked, obviously knowing the man who greeted them.

'Indeed, sir. I would gladly row you across, but the next job is owed to John Ferguson, so he will perform that service,' Paul said, gesturing to one of his colleagues.

'Aye, sir and madam, it will be my pleasure, if you would care to step this way,' and led them to the end of the jetty, where they stepped carefully down into the waiting boat.

'Thank you, wherryman,' Steven said politely as he and Joanne sat alongside each other.

'Hold on securely madam,' John Ferguson said as he used the oars to push them clear of the jetty.

As the wherryman rowed towards midstream, they were more exposed to the cold January breeze. Thankfully, it was a dry sunny day, but the cold air bit into them, causing Joanne instinctively to move closer to Steven, seeking shelter and warmth. He glanced over to find her close at his side, realising she might have underestimated the weather.

'Miss Joanne, may I offer some protection?' and he lifted his arm to invite her closer. Without reply, Joanne smiled and moved closer, so their bodies were connected, her head resting against his chest, and he moved his arm around her back, his hand gently resting on her shoulder. She immediately felt warmer, sheltered from the cold wind, and thought she would enjoy the river crossing if it could last longer.

Safely reaching the south bank, getting onto dry land was more difficult as there were fewer jetties allowing transfer without stepping through the lapping water. There was also the danger of stepping off the boat and sinking in mud. Fortunately, John Ferguson knew the best places to deliver passengers without the water flowing over the tops of their boots, or danger of them sinking in the mud to their knees. He rowed the boat into the riverbank, where it came to a halt.

'There you are, miss. If you step up to the front of the boat, I think you can avoid both water and mud,' and he climbed out of the boat, pulling it four feet up the riverbank, then held out a hand to assist his passengers.

Steven led Joanne up the shingle border of the river and onto a grassy bank. They stood at the edge of a small fenced field, consisting of grass and a large vegetable garden, with a small house at the far end. A footpath followed the fence alongside the field and, as they passed the vegetable garden, Steven was impressed with how well-kept it looked. There were a few crops growing, possibly some winter turnips or parsnips, with the rest of the earth turned over and left ready for spring planting. Joanne noticed his examination of the garden.

'Are you interested in farming, Major?' she asked, curious to find out a little of his background.

'Yes, my family has a farm in Hertfordshire, Miss Joanne. I enjoyed growing up there and tending the vegetable garden when I was a boy. But that seems an age ago now that my life is soldiering.'

'Does this house impress you with its tendering of the land?'

'Yes, it is a fine-looking vegetable garden, well organised and ready for spring planting. I hope the winter stays mild for them and does not continue into March.'

As they walked past the house, an elderly woman emerged for the purpose of collecting some wood from a shelter to the side.

'Good day to you, madam,' Steven called.

'Good day to you both,' she replied, 'It is a cold day to be out walking, you must be sweethearts!' she added with a toothless smile and returned into the house.

Joanne could not supress a smile and blushed.

'Well, we had better press on to avoid a chill and further comment,' Steven said with a smile of his own.

Just past the small house, a footpath followed the line of the river, so they turned left and followed it eastwards. Every 100 feet or so, another house would appear with its own garden, and this continued for a quarter of a mile until the footpath became a road known simply as Upper Ground, which Steven knew would lead them to the district of Southwark. Despite the change from footpath to road, the use of the land did not immediately change, with homes and gardens on the river side, and farms the other side. The density of the buildings increased, and farm fields disappeared as Upper Ground passed by houses, a church, tavern and blacksmith's workshop. Then set back from the road they were alongside a space where the remains of a large building littered the ground. It was clear from what was left that it was circular in design.

'What was this place, Major,' Joanne asked.

'This is where the Globe Theatre stood.'

'Ah, yes, I have heard of this theatre.'

'It was closed by Parliament in 1642 and demolished a couple of years later.'

'For what reason, Major?' Joanne asked.

Steven paused, considering that in different company he would be wise to be circumspect with his words, but with Joanne he could speak openly.

'Our Puritan rulers believe theatres are places of licentiousness, drunken behaviour and sin. So, they closed theatres for our moral benefit, Miss Joanne.'

'Do you agree with those measures, Major? Do you think Parliament closing theatres would make people more moral?'

Steven glanced over his shoulder, lest someone might overhear their conversation, but there was no one to hear.

'Well, Miss Joanne, if I am honest, I would say "no," but I could face grave consequences if I stated this publicly. The Lord Protector and I were both impressed with the views of you and your uncle two months ago, and they reflect the feelings of many, who feel that Parliament has become too prescriptive.'

'Prescriptive?' Joanne asked.

'Apologies for not speaking as plainly as you did, Miss Joanne. Imposing rules, telling folk how they should live, dear lady,' Steven replied with a smile.

'Prescriptive? I see, and that included telling them theatres were bad for them,' Joanne said and looked back at the remains of the once great theatre.

'Let us press on, we have some distance to walk, and I do not want us to be chided by your uncle.' They turned away from where the Globe had stood, and continued eastwards through Southwark. For a few minutes neither spoke. Joanne thought about what Steven said and sympathised with the sentiments he articulately expressed.

As the housing and other buildings became more crowded, Steven knew they would pass through parts of Southwark that were frequented by cutpurses, street women and other less desirable company, but he thought they should be safe from danger on a Sunday lunchtime. He was correct regarding thieves and men who might cause harm. However, he was not familiar with the brazenness of women in doorways and alleys at all hours of the day, selling themselves so they could eat. To get to the road that crossed the river over London Bridge, they cut through a small lane to the south of the cathedral. The narrow thoroughfare was always shaded and dark, even at midday, and stood in a doorway were three women wearing less than would be considered decent.

'Hello, my loves, what are you two lovebirds doing down here? Lost your way?' one of the three said as Joanne was within three feet. She was startled and stepped back, causing laughter amongst the three women. Steven instinctively put his arm around her shoulders to protect her. 'Don't worry, darling, we ain't going to steal your boyfriend! Not unless he chooses to visit us...' one of the others said, resulting in more coarse laughter.

'Excuse us, ladies,' Steven said, 'we are just making our way to the bridge.'

'Ooh, what a gentleman. A proper gentleman she's got there,' the third replied. 'Just keep walking through there and turn left at the end of the lane.'

'Thank you, ladies,' Steven said and taking his arm from around her shoulders and placing it through Joanne's, he escorted her along the middle of the lane. Once they were safely at the end and onto a wider well-lit road that led up to the bridge, he felt able to speak.

'I am most sorry you had to experience that, Miss Joanne.'

'Oh, Major Flain, I was just surprised, not afraid. I have grown up in a tavern and am familiar with women of their trade.' She was flattered that the major thought she might not have encountered such women before, and grateful for their approach as it resulted in him holding her close again, just as he had in the wherry. Walking to the end of the lane arm-in-arm made the walk more pleasurable.

Crossing the bridge, they were suddenly amongst a throng of people, bustling between the houses and shops perched above the Thames. It was noisy and again they joined arms for security and to avoid separation.

'I cannot believe it could be so busy on a Sunday, Major, as if it were market day.'

Steven smiled, enjoying the mass of humanity and the close proximity of his escort.

'Can I ask something of you, Miss Joanne?'

'Of course, Major.'

'Would you call me Steven?'

'I might find that difficult, sir, because of your rank and place in society.'

'What do you mean?'

'I am just a tavern maid, sir,' she said modestly, wondering if this encounter was foolish, and looked down.

Steven was annoyed but did not want to ruin what had been a most pleasurable hour.

'Do you understand, sir?' There she was, doing it again.

'If you do not refer to me as Steven, I could refuse to visit you, but it would be lunacy to deny this pleasure because of your propriety,' he said with a smile, which made Joanne feel a little more comfortable.

'Good, so you will just have to tolerate me calling you Major, or sir,' she said with a warm smile, placing her arm back through his, and they resumed their navigation across the bridge.

Once across the river they turned left on Thames Street walking westwards, before turning right up Bennet's Hill. It was a short climb uphill to bring them to the tall imposing spire of St Paul's church, where they paused to admire the great medieval house of worship.

'It is a wonderful building,' Joanne said, staring up at the gothic spire, 'but parts of it seem to have been damaged.'

'Yes, I believe this building is over 300 years-old, and there has been a church here for 1,000 years since the first English Christians. But sadly, parts of it have been damaged since the war, as all vestiges of catholic worship were destroyed,' Steven explained.

'That seems most sad, Major.'

'Yes, it does. Our country has suffered from so much intolerance this last 100 years since the last Henry,' he replied, sharing Joanne's sentiments.

From St Paul's it was an almost straight road back to Charing Cross, along Ludgate Street, which became Fleet Street, which then became the Strand. They slowed their pace that last mile, both realising they were nearing the end of their walk, eventually arriving at the end of the Strand, just minutes from the Three Tuns.

'Well, here we are, Miss Joanne,' Steven said as they reached the tavern. 'May I thank you for allowing me to walk with you. It was a great pleasure to be in your company today. I do hope it was pleasant for you too.' They stood still, neither wishing to end their encounter, neither knowing an appropriate parting. After a few moments, Joanne took the initiative.

'Major, it was my pleasure too,' and she leaned forward kissing him lightly on his cheek. Without more words, she turned and disappeared into the tavern. Steven watched her and gently touched his cheek, where moments earlier her lips had touched his face.

'Thank you, Joanne Aker,' he said to himself, then turned back towards Charing Cross.

February 1654

Major Steven Flain walked through the great door, where he was met by Jonathan Litchfield, Cromwell's trusted aide. He was a tall angular man dressed in the black robes of a scholar or man of the law, with a black cloth cap and no indication of any military connection.

'Good day to you, Major Flain.'

'Good day to you, Mr Litchfield,' Steven Flain replied.

'The Lord Protector will be pleased you have come so promptly. He is eager for you to meet a distinguished servant of the Commonwealth. But I will not say anymore, lest there are ears about us, so I shall let our master explain.'

'Yes, Mr Litchfield,' an intrigued Steven replied and followed him through the Palace of Westminster corridors to Cromwell's private quarters.

Inside the familiar room where Steven had attended several meetings with Cromwell, he found his master sat at the large table that dominated the room. Alongside Cromwell sat another man, dressed like Jonathan Litchfield in the long black robes of a scholar or lawyer. Both men looked up as Steven and Jonathan entered the room, but Steven was immediately aware that there was something different about the unknown man. Whereas Cromwell looked directly at them, the other man's head was turned slightly to the right, as if someone else was there. Steven then noticed a glazed look in his eyes and realised the man was blind.

'Ah, excellent, Major Flain. Thank you for coming at short notice. Please, sit with us,' Cromwell said.

'Yes, sir. I came as quickly as I could,' Steven replied, with a respectful nod.

'Major Flain, I would like you to meet a very distinguished scholar, who helps me in a number of ways, particularly with regards to foreign correspondence,' Cromwell said. As he spoke the scholarly blind man stood up and held out his hand across the table, and Cromwell introduced him. 'This is John Milton.'

'Good day, Major Flain, I have heard much about you from the Lord Protector.'

'It is my privilege and honour, sir,' Steven replied. He had heard of this man, an academic, a poet, who had been given a position working for the Council of State after the Civil War and now for Cromwell himself. The unusual nature of such an appointment was what made Milton's position in government widely known amongst army officers, many expressing surprise and derision, 'a bloody poet in the government,' being a commonly held view. Apart from that, Steven would have to admit to not knowing any more about this man and why he was employed in government. He was about to find out. Steven shook hands with Milton, the four men sat at the large table that dominated the room and could speak openly in private.

'Major Flain,' Cromwell continued, 'Mr Milton's official title is Secretary of Foreign Tongues, which may sound rather sinister, but do not fear, it has nothing to do with witchery.' This was met with a loud 'Ha!' by the great scholar. 'That title is because he has these last five years played an important role in writing letters and pamphlets on behalf of the Commonwealth. He has command of six or seven languages,' Cromwell added.

'Eight languages, to be precise, Oliver,' Milton said, turning his head slightly but still not directly facing any of the other three.

'Apologies, John,' Cromwell said with a smile, and moved his left hand to touch Milton's right hand, a gesture of friendly reassurance.

'Ah, Oliver, it is of no consequence,' Milton replied, and at first Steven was surprised to hear someone refer to Cromwell using his Christian name, but then realised the two men spoke to each other as equals, even friends.

After further explanation of his role in government and

that he had been blind for nearly two years, Cromwell wanted to get to the business of the meeting.

'Steven, I think we may have a solution to the problem of what to do with our dissenting friends, if I may call them that here, which I could not amongst the likes of Charles Hadleigh.'

'Sir?' Steven replied.

'I have been confiding in John over the issue of dissenters and their persecution. This has become pressing after our visit to the Three Tuns tavern and our conversation with Mr Wiggett and his niece, Miss Aker,' Cromwell said.

'Yes, sir, Steven replied, his attention more focused after mention of Joanne.

'John has had an idea, which may be something we could consider if things become too dangerous for our 'friends' here in London. Would you care to explain, John?'

'Certainly, Oliver. Major Flain, I have great respect for men and women who challenge the authority of the established church. My father was disinherited by my grandfather because he converted from Catholicism to the Church of England. I myself chose to be a Puritan, and I find the teachings of Calvin's Presbyterians too authoritarian.'

'I see, sir,' Steven replied, uncertain where this conversation was heading, but willing to listen if it led to the safety of Joanne.

'Almost thirty years ago, when I was studying at Cambridge University, I became friends with a man named Roger Williams. Have you heard of him, Major Flain?' Milton asked.

'No, sir,' Steven replied, slightly embarrassed by his ignorance, expecting to hear that Roger Williams was a major figure in the government.

'Roger was a brilliant scholar, Major. He could speak many languages and taught me Dutch, in return for me helping him learn Hebrew. He also took holy orders, qualifying him to become a minister in the Church of England. But before doing so, he became a Puritan, turning his back on the established church, like myself and Oliver,' Milton said and put his hand on that of his friend.

'Yes, sir,' Steven said, intrigued by the connection between the three men and how this was relevant to John Wiggett, Joanne and the other dissenters.

'You are probably wondering how this pertains to your so-called dissenting friends,' Milton said. 'Well, dissatisfied with the way the Church of England was moving in the period when Charles closed Parliament after 1629, Roger decided to go to the New World, joining our Puritan brothers in Massachusetts.'

'I see, sir,' Steven said, at least understanding why he'd never heard of Roger Williams, and beginning to guess where their dissenting friends might go for safety.

'Once in the Americas, Roger continued to develop his ideas on freedom of conscience, the issue that pre-occupies so many good men and women here in England. Men and women like Quakers. This brought Roger into conflict with the governors of the Massachusetts colony, because he advocated the separation of church and state, which did not sit well with the government of that colony.'

Steven simply nodded, not quite understanding what 'separation of church and state' meant, allowing the blind scholar to continue.

'As a result, Roger Williams was expelled from the Massachusetts Colony in 1636 for what they considered to be sedition and heresy,' Milton explained.

'Does it sound familiar, Major?' Cromwell asked.

'Indeed, it does, sir.'

'Roger established a new colony at a place he named Providence Plantation in Rhode Island, which he wanted to make a refuge for the liberty of conscience and, dissatisfied with the intolerance shown by Puritans, he converted again, this time to become a Baptist. As a result, Providence, Rhode Island, has become a successful colony, attracting dissenters from different sects seeking freedom of conscience. I correspond with my old friend and his ideas have progressed further to argue that the state should not be concerned with the Ten Commandments that refer to the relationship between man and God. So, it should not be a crime to commit blasphemy, Sabbath-breaking, or idolatry. These things are a matter for a man's conscience, between him and God. Roger argues the state should be concerned with acts that break commandments between people, like murder, theft, adultery, lying. This leads to a separation of church and state,' Milton explained.

'This sounds like much of what dissenters here ask for, sir,' Steven said, grateful for the scholar's explanation.

A smile appeared on Cromwell's face. 'Precisely, Major. There are stark parallels,' he said.

'May I ask a question, sir?' Steven asked.

'Yes, of course, Major.'

'Why do the established churches wish to oppose a man's freedom of conscience?'

Cromwell looked at him with a resigned look. 'A very pertinent question, Major, which we can perhaps discuss over a cup of ale in John Wiggett's tavern. However, I fear eternity would not be time enough to explain this matter,' and his answer was met with a nod from Steven.

Milton smiled. 'Major Flain, one of Roger's many quotes, of which I am most fond is, "Forced worship stinks in God's nostrils." He has a wonderful way of putting things in simple terms, do you agree, Oliver?'

Yes, John,' Cromwell replied, grateful for his friend's contribution. 'Perhaps we should invite him back to address the vipers I have to listen to in Parliament.'

Milton laughed again, enjoying the meeting. 'He would certainly say things they may not wish to hear, Oliver.' Then glancing slightly to Steven's left he asked, 'What do you say, Major?'

'I begin to understand, sir. Thank you, this has been most illuminating. Am I correct in thinking Providence might be a place of refuge for dissenters from here, should their freedom be in doubt?' Steven asked.

'I believe you may well be correct, Major,' Cromwell replied with a wry smile.

'How would we facilitate a plan to achieve this, sir?'

'Well, it would certainly involve the requisition of a ship and employing the services of a captain and crew. Obviously, this must be kept privy to as few persons as possible. Whilst I am commander of the army and navy, I am mindful of malcontents in this place, so beyond we four I will involve perhaps just one trusted third party to make the arrangements on our behalf, keeping them ignorant of its purpose.'

'This could be problematic, Oliver,' Milton said.

'Yes, John. It is a delicate matter, but not one, I believe, beyond our capabilities.'

'How frequently do ships sail for those colonies, sir?' Steven asked.

'A good question, Steven. I am informed that after Easter, ships will sail for the American colonies each week through to the end of summer, such is the increase in trade across the ocean.'

John Milton nodded, adding, 'It sounds to me that you have been busy with this matter already, Oliver.'

'I could not possibly comment, John,' Cromwell replied with a smile, which the poet could not see, but the sentiment was conveyed with a gentle slap on his back.

March 1654

Laura squeezed through the crowd into the town hall, followed by Margaret, where they found spaces on the wooden bench that was the third row of seats for the public to witness the trial. This placed them down one side of the long hall, from where they could view proceedings. To their right at the end of the hall was a raised platform with a long table, behind which were several men in sombre Puritan dress, but in the middle of them was an empty chair, almost throne-like, with a high back and solid arms. It did not take much imagination to realise this is where the commissioner would sit as judge. In front of Laura and Margaret a young woman with her head bowed sat on a chair in the middle of the floor, facing the platform and long table. Behind the seated young woman stood two soldiers holding their six feet long halberds upright. The other side of the hall facing the defendant and the five rows of public observers was another table at which sat several notaries and scribes.

As Laura and the other public observers were gazing at the forlorn girl, a small door in the corner of the hall opened and through it walked a tall man in the same Puritan dress as the other three sat behind the table, but a fine lace collar denoted wealth, power, or perhaps both. He stepped up onto the platform and took his seat without fuss or ceremony. There was no 'All rise,' or any other pronouncement, but when Commissioner Godswill Brown eventually stood to address everyone the hall was silent.

'We are here to witness the delivery of the law of Parliament and God,' he announced, so no one in the hall could be unaware of the purpose. 'The woman before us, Susan Bounty, has been charged with breaking the Adultery Act of 1650 and God's holy commandment. Before any witnesses are heard and evidence is considered, we would ask you, Susan Bounty, what you have to say in your defence.'

Susan looked up at the men at the table on the raised platform. 'I am sorry, sir,' was all she could offer, hoping honesty might bring clemency, but she was to be disappointed.

'Are you guilty, or innocent of the charge, Susan Bounty?' Godswill Brown asked, thinking to himself this was not going to take long.

'Sir, I have sinned, for which I ask forgiveness,' the young woman replied softly, causing the four men to lean forward to hear clearly, whilst the forty or so members of the public looked at each other for confirmation of what they thought they had heard.

'Let us be clear, Susan Bounty. Did you commit the sins and crimes of fornication and adultery with William Fogg, a married man from Bristol?' Brown asked loud and clear.

Susan had glanced down after her previous reply, placing her hands on her protruding belly in which her and William Fogg's child was growing. This had been seen by everyone in the hall making the first part of the commissioner's question rhetorical. But the second part was yet to be confirmed. Laura fixed her stare on Susan, willing her to speak words that would mitigate her condition. If William Fogg was the father, Susan must say it was rape, her honour taken by the married man against her will. 'Say it, Susan,' Laura thought, 'say he forced you, he hurt you, and shed tears as you speak. Or say the father is not Fogg. Say the father is a young man from another town or village. Fornication would be punished less severely than adultery. You will live and your child will have a mother.' Laura's thoughts were pounding in her head. She wanted to call out the counsel she could offer the young woman, but that was impossible. Instead she sat in silence and listened to Susan seal her own fate.

'Yes, sir. I am sorry, sir.'

Six words were all she spoke, her naivety and innocence causing a stir amongst the five rows of public observers. Their disbelief preceded a collective sadness, as each member of the audience realised the drama would be short-lived, six words bringing a speedy conclusion. Laura leaned forward, covering her face with her hands, not wanting to see what her ears had heard. As she waited with everyone else for what seemed like an age for Godswill Brown's reply, Laura's thoughts turned to her own beginnings and her mother, Mary, who forty-one years earlier was in the same predicament as the girl, Susan Bounty, sat before them facing a possible death sentence. Laura's mother, Mary, had fallen to the charms of an older man in the late summer of 1612, but was cast out from her home in Falmouth by her father, who would have 'no bastards in my house,' as Mary later recounted to Laura. Sitting there, waiting for the Puritan Commissioner to speak, Laura realised Mary had never told her if her natural father was married. 'Perhaps he was not married, so I would be the product of simple fornication, not adultery. My mother would have escaped a death sentence here today.' But then she thought, 'Is it likely her father would have cast her out if the father was not married? Mary was the daughter of a respectable family and she was attractive. Surely my grandfather would have forced them to marry. My mother would not have been the first young woman at the altar with a child growing in her womb,' she thought. Then it occurred to Laura that her mother had never told her their family name in Falmouth, and it had never mattered to Laura, as she was raised with the name Baddow, after her mother married a widower with two young children, who became her brother and sister. But before that, the heavily pregnant Mary had wandered into the village of Mevagissey in Cornwell, where her fate was different to that facing Susan Bounty. Mary was taken in by the local vestry and placed in the local poor house, where with the assistance of local women she gave birth to Laura. It was hardly a privileged start in life, but Laura new she was fortunate to have been born in a kinder England, before the Civil War, before a Puritan Parliament, and before their morality laws. Then her thoughts were interrupted by the Puritan commissioner.

'Susan Bounty, you have admitted to your guilt. Breaking the laws of God and Parliament through fornication and adultery, your crimes are punishable by death.' A groan from the audience caused Godswill Brown to pause. 'You will be held in the gaol here in Honiton and allowed to give birth, as your unborn bastard is not guilty of your sin. God will forgive your infant, but you will have to wait to find out if he will forgive you. After you have given birth and suckled the infant, you will be taken to the main square, where you will be hanged.'

Susan did not speak, traumatised by the sentence. Her face was ashen as she placed her hands on the protrusion of her unborn child. Again, Laura wanted to call out in protest, but her throat was dry, and no words formed. Instead a tear fell down her cheek as her stare remained fixed on the girl. In front of Laura and slightly to the right Anne Bounty was sobbing uncontrollably and began to wail, calling out, 'Dear God, Susan, no!'

Susan Bounty turned her head on recognising the voice and finally lost composure, 'Mother! Please help me!' The sombre, calm atmosphere of the hall was shattered by a sudden outpouring of emotion, as the pregnant girl stood up and attempted to get to her mother. But the two soldiers barred her path, each grabbing an arm. Susan's mother was distraught and continued to wail as women around her tried to provide comfort. Godswill Brown stood up, realising he had to show authority and control, lest there was a serious challenge to the law being seen to be done.

'Guards, take the prisoner back to the gaol!' Brown shouted and was relieved to see four more soldiers come forward from the back of the hall to ensure order, but there was no uprising from the audience, just a resigned sadness at the sight of Parliament's will being delivered. Susan was sobbing as the meaning of the sentence was finally realised, but despite turning her head back towards the benches she was not allowed any further contact with her mother, as she was marched out

of the hall by the six soldiers. After a lull the audience from
the public gallery followed with no more than murmurs. Left
behind were no more than half a dozen women. Three of them
were consoling Susan's mother, whose head was buried in their
embrace. Laura looked on, her heart breaking for the poor
woman, before turning to Margaret, who said, 'Come, cousin.
Let us leave this sad place.'

April 1654

Inside Parliament Cromwell had to listen for what seemed an eternity as the debate raged over what to do about the rising clamour for reform. The anger seemed tangible, as if it could be touched, as MPs from all over England, Wales and Scotland demanded action be taken over the blasphemy and sedition of agitators, whether they be former Levellers and Diggers, or even Quakers campaigning for change.

'This outrage must be stopped now!'

'Arrest them and send them to the Tower!'

'Servitude in the colonies!'

'Put their heads on pikes on London Bridge for everyone to see!'

The calls rained down from the two sides of the Commons, and all Cromwell could do was maintain a face that gave no indication of his sympathy for men wanting reform. 'Dear God,' he thought, 'these self-serving men of wealth would arrest half of England's army,' and for a moment closed his eyes. Eventually the noise abated, and the debate closed with a promise from the Lord Protector that action would be taken. An hour later Cromwell was pleased to be outside with the young officer he had come to trust and listened to for advice on the mood of his men.

'Major Flain, I fear for our friends in Barnet, and the two Welshmen, who might soon be in mortal danger.'

'Yes, sir. Is there anything we can do?'

'Not about taking action to quash dissent. I feel my hands are tied. This title, Lord Protector of the Commonwealth of England, Scotland and Ireland, sounds grand, but I am unable to protect these men. Their actions are contrary to the law, and worse, they anger men of property and power. There is going to be an investigation by servants of Parliament to uncover blasphemy, heresy and sedition, Major. They want to make an example of men like our friends.' He looked out from a terrace to the side of the Palace of Westminster, across the Thames and towards the east, where the Tower awaited the agitators who challenged the MPs in the house behind him.

'Is there nothing to be done, sir?' Steven asked. He was aware of what it was to which Cromwell referred. MPs were determined to crush the call for reform that would leave them poorer, and they were determined to make an example of Quakers, that might now include former Levellers, and particularly Diggers, whenever and wherever they could be found. The suspicion of agitators gathering at inns and taverns across London had proved to be justified, he had witnessed it himself at the Swan and Three Tuns, where he feared for the safety of Joanne and her uncle. Cromwell explained that secret guards had been readied to raid a number of hostelries and seize miscreants, and Steven understood Cromwell could not be seen to side with the agitators for fear of another schism in Parliament.

Both men stared down at the riverbank, where several wherrymen gathered to talk. These men were to be seen every day waiting for passengers who employed them for the purpose of transport, usually east towards the City, where commerce was conducted, to the Tower itself, and sometimes past London Bridge to where ships waited to sail to a plethora of foreign destinations. Cromwell wondered if employing wherrymen to get to ships sailing away from these shores might soon be an urgent option for some reformers.

'I cannot oppose Parliament on this matter, Major,' Cromwell said with a resigned sigh. He realised his sympathy for these men wanting reforms, particularly their call for freedom of conscience to worship a common Christian God, was at odds with his position to uphold the law.

'I understand, sir,' Steven replied with sincere sympathy, knowing the prospects for Davies, Evans, Martin and Odlin did not look bright if they did not do something. Worse, he could not bear to think of Joanne's treatment in somewhere like the Tower, where torture awaited those who refused to confess.

As they spoke the wherrymen burst into activity as a group of men emerged from the Palace of Westminster. Marching with purpose the men of importance called to the three wherrymen as they approached, which could not be clearly heard on the terrace but could be guessed at as various destinations. The caps of the wherrymen were tipped and within seconds the passengers were in three boats being rowed away from the riverbank towards midstream where the current was stronger and would assist their haste eastwards.

Pausing to observe the seamless operation, Cromwell and Flain watched with admiration, and Cromwell turned to the Major.

'I cannot defy the law, Steven, but perhaps we need to take action to precipitate an escape for our friends before it is delivered, if required, as we discussed.'

Steven turned to face the Lord Protector, remembering the meeting they had shared with John Milton two months earlier.

'And that may have to include John Wiggett and Joanne Aker, Steven,' Cromwell said, knowing the young officer had an affection for the young woman.

'I understand, sir. Their safety is the priority consideration, sir.'

Cromwell had word sent to Elizabeth that he would sleep in his private quarters in the Palace of Westminster that night, not because he was unwell, simply that he had business to attend to first thing in the morning. It was a warm evening and he was pleased to have some time to think as he sat on the terrace looking down towards the Thames, with just two of his personal guards in attendance. He ate his supper alone, with his guards standing sentry outside his quarters, and before retiring he was able to read, something that had become a luxury with his responsibilities as commander of the army and then Head of State. Perhaps it was the influence of the day's work and the problem of what to do about the dissenters, but he found himself reaching for the work of his friend and confidante, John Milton. *Areopagitica* was a speech written ten years earlier and Milton presented a copy of it to his new master when Cromwell became Lord Protector. The speech had become famous in learned circles and even a commercial success, supplementing its writer's income.

'I wrote this during the Civil War, Oliver, at a time when some were arguing for censorship and against freedom of speech. Men will do extreme things in time of war, but these rights should be protected. I want you to have this, Oliver, and think on these issues carefully,' Milton had said a year earlier, the words still clear in Cromwell's memory.

He had been intending to read it for some time, so that evening seemed an appropriate opportunity. On the table was an ornate glass decanter that had belonged to his predecessor as Head of State. His aide, Michael Coleman, had filled it with port, which he would not empty, but was not averse to sipping modestly. The warm evening outside had turned cooler, so he had his aide light the fire before being dismissed for the night.

'Good night to you, Michael. Thank you for your assistance.'

'Thank you, sir, and a good night to you.'

He then settled into the large leather chair by the fire, with the port at arm's length, and started reading. As he did his thoughts were of the dissenters, as well as John Wiggett and his niece, Joanne.

An hour or so later, he said a brief prayer and climbed into bed. He felt well, relieved the night fevers and chills that had afflicted him for some years seemed, mercifully, to have spared him of late. There would be no dreams, but for a while his thoughts lingered on what to do about the dissenters. Perhaps it was the influence of the transcript of Milton's speech about freedom of speech and censorship, but he resolved to do something that might save some from prosecution and worse.

'Tomorrow, I must speak to Robert Blake,' he said to himself and closed his eyes.

May 1654

Susan Bounty was led through the town from the poor house, where she had been kept under lock and key since the birth, to the market square in the shadow of the church spire. It was late afternoon and the summer sun was moving across the sky towards the west, where Susan should have sailed once she knew she was with child. A new life in the colonies was an option that offered a chance of life, but it was too late. The infant girl she carried in her arms, held close to her breast, yawned with tiredness having been suckled in a dingy room in the poor house, satisfied by her mother's milk and drifting into a deep sleep. The nineteen-year-old mother glanced down, knowing these were the last minutes she would know of her child, her last minutes on this earth.

Turning the corner by the baker's house, Susan looked up to see the wooden construction that had been erected since the previous day. A platform raised four feet from the ground, with six steps to the side. Stood on the platform was the gallows, from which a rope with a noose hung. Five feet below the noose was a small stool. She shuffled through the crowd that had gathered, the path forged by four godly soldiers, two either side of her, following a solemn Puritan commissioner.

Susan knew what faced her, but it was only when she saw the noose that would squeeze the last breath from her body, that she was filled with fear. Her legs felt hollow and she might have collapsed but for a maternal instinct to support her child. However, her stride shortened and she slowed, causing the four soldiers to stop. Godswill Brown sensed his prisoner and escort were not close behind as the eyes of the crowd turned further back than where they had been just behind himself. He stopped and turned to see the young woman shuffling, almost at a standstill.

'Come girl, the fate you have brought upon yourself by your immorality stands before you.'

There was no kindness, nor was there malice, just a coldness as he stated a fact the crowd had gathered to see.

Susan resumed the walk to the platform and scaffold, arriving at the steps after no more than a minute. As she took the first step she began to tremble, fear and an awareness of what was happening causing her to feel cold and weak, but she kept hold of her daughter with both arms making her balance on the steps uncertain. She would not be allowed to stumble or fall as two of the soldiers moved closer to escort her up onto the platform, whilst the other two stood at the bottom of the steps to stop anyone who might think they could interrupt the law and justice of Puritan England. Godswill Brown stood on the platform, alongside a large strong man wearing a mask to hide his identity. Behind Susan and the two soldiers a woman, dressed in black and wearing a headcover, solemnly followed them up onto the platform.

'This woman has confessed and been found guilty of adultery by a court of law. Parliament is unequivocal, as is the Bible. Adultery is punishable by death and we are here to witness the law of God and Parliament.' Godswill Brown spoke to the people of Honiton and others who had come to see the delivery of Parliament's justice.

'Do you have anything to say Susan Bounty, before you leave this world and face God's judgement?'

Susan looked at the cold face of the Puritan commissioner who had brought her arrest and trial. Then she looked down at the innocent face of her child and out across the crowded market square filled with faces whose eyes were fixed on her. Quiet had fallen as everyone listened to hear the girl's last words.

'Sir, I have sinned, for which I am sorry and have confessed. Please, sir, I beg you, for my life and that of my daughter. Please show mercy.'

Finally, the tears the crowd had come to see streamed down her cheeks. Many of them had seen an execution; just three weeks earlier John Evans had been hanged for the murder of his neighbour, after their years-long feud was settled following the consumption of excessive alcohol. His sentence was handed out for two acts of immorality in the eyes of a Puritan Parliament. However, this was different; the death by hanging of a pretty young woman for adultery. She would hang for committing sins of the flesh with a married man. The presence of the baby in her arms, born just days before, was all the evidence they needed, but alongside the ghoulish interest of some men who could barely conceal their pleasure at the macabre entertainment, there was also the pained look of others. Women were sorry for the girl who had simply made a mistake by allowing herself to be seduced by the charm and promises of an older man. 'The poor girl. What was she thinking?' thought more than one of the older women who had warned their own daughters of such dangers.

'That I cannot do, and now you must pay for your sin against God, and your crime against the law of the Commonwealth of England. Mistress Jenkins! Guards!' The commissioner's call was met by the two guards and the solemn woman closing in on Susan. She was powerless as the older woman took the baby from her, and the guards each held an arm behind her back as the masked executioner tied rope around her wrists.

'Sir, please, I beg you. Please let me live. I do not want to die!' Susan screamed, causing gasps from members of the crowd.

As the older woman stepped back, a cloth was tied around Susan's head by the executioner, covering her eyes. With the two soldiers the masked man lifted Susan without difficulty off the ground and onto the stool beneath the noose, which he pulled down and slipped over her head so that it rested like a thick necklace around her neck. Then, with a gentle touch that belied his size he tightened the noose, before moving to the upright to pull the rope taut and tying it to the post. Susan could feel the tension in the rope, causing her to stand straight, her neck slightly bent. No more words were said, the noose prevented Susan from speaking, but her tears continued to seep down from behind the cloth covering her eyes.

Godswill Brown had nothing else to add, he just turned to the executioner and nodded. The man in the mask moved over to stand behind Susan, who he could hear whimpering, but he could not let her distract him as he focused on the stool, kicking it away with force. Everyone in the crowd gasped as the girl's body dropped and hanged in the air, her legs kicking for what seemed like minutes, but was less than one, until she was still, hanging limply.

The four adults standing on the platform knew they had to remain until it was certain the girl was dead, after which her body would be loaded into a cart, to be taken to a pauper's grave. Having seen what they had come to witness, members of the crowd began to turn and leave. For a moment quietness enveloped the square, until it was punctured by Susan's baby crying for her mother's milk.

Laura had stood at the rear of the assembled crowd, partly resigned, partly ashamed that she had been unable to affect in any way the outcome of Susan's trial. She would rather have returned to her home close to Sidmouth, but she could not leave the young girl, cruelly judged by Parliament and its commissioners, alone on her last day. She had wanted to call out to Susan, letting her know she was not alone, Laura Longbow was there in the crowd and wanted to hold her hand as she left this earth. She wanted to reassure the girl that the men who judged her were wrong, that she would be in heaven that day, and that her daughter would be cared for on this earth. But when the time came she couldn't speak or call out. Laura could only stand in silence as the final moments of Susan's life were played out. Now it was over, tears flowed from her eyes as she witnessed justice being served, and her mouth spoke thoughts she would have done well to hide, 'Damn these Puritans, damn this Parliament, and damn you, William Fogg.'

14th June 1654

Cromwell was seated at a long wooden table, behind which was another table with various pieces of stationery; blank parchments, quills, thick volumes, his Seal of State with a bowl of red wax, candles, two jugs or water and cups. This space at the end of a darkened room was where he conducted much of the affairs of state, received official visits and private ones to hear personal appeals. Major Flain stood at one end of the table, whilst at the other end stood Cromwell's aide, Jonathan Litchfield. Cromwell's most trusted aide who was not in the army stood sentry. With Steven at the other end of the table, the Lord Protector felt most comfortable with these two men in whom he had complete faith.

'That damned pest, Hadleigh, will be here soon, gentleman. And I fear I must comply with his wish to arrest agitators, who have been identified as collaborating with former Diggers, True Levellers, Levellers, or whatever they are now calling themselves, Jonathan?' Cromwell said, exasperated and uncertain which name was appropriate.

'Sir,' Jonathan said, 'I believe if we are to be accurate, the Diggers liked to be called True Levellers, but there are no more of their little colonies surviving in England. The Levellers were a different group, and whilst John Lilburne still campaigns, they have largely disappeared, their ambitions failing to be realised.' Litchfield was always polite and precise, an academic, along with John Milton, one of the few non-military men he could tolerate.

'Yes, yes, I know all of that, Jonathan,' Cromwell snapped impatiently, 'It was I who crushed the maniac Diggers, or whatever they would call themselves.' Cromwell valued the counsel of the learned scholar, but sometimes progressing with business could be more lengthy than necessary with his pedantry.

'Excuse me, sir. I was just clarifying,' Jonathan said

apologetically.

At the other end of the table, Steven had to suppress a smile at the exchange between the two, the nature of which he had witnessed before, knowing Cromwell would soon forgive and forget.

'Very good, Jonathan, I know, I know. Here, sit with me please. I will need your assistance,' Cromwell said, gesturing for his aide to sit beside him. 'Steven, when Sir Charles arrives, would you go out to greet him and tell him to enter when called, and then stand by the door whilst Jonathan and I listen to his prating.'

'Yes, sir,' Steven replied.

'If he has the names of persons we know and wish to protect, we may have to take clandestine action, Major,'

'Yes, sir, Steven said again, this time more alert, realising those 'persons' could include John and Joanne. He had no other duty to perform, so stood at ease to the side as Cromwell and Jonathan discussed a tax that was being considered to raise finance for the purpose of building more ships to fight the Dutch, but their words passed over Steven as his thoughts turned to Joanne and a threat to her liberty. Meeting her had brought him pleasure he had not known for some time, but if it might lead to her being in danger, he would rather he had never taken his master into the Three Tuns six months earlier, thereby avoiding the friendship that followed.

After some minutes had passed the sound of footsteps could be heard approaching along the corridor leading to Cromwell's office. His guards the other side of the door would stop any visitors, regardless of rank or position, signifying their arrival with two loud bangs on the door with the hilt of a sword, and that was what followed the footsteps. The discussion of tax and building ships was interrupted, causing both Cromwell and Litchfield to look up from the table.

'Thank you, Steven,' Cromwell said. The major walked over to the door, which he opened and passed through, closing it behind him.

'The Lord Protector will be ready for you in a minute, Sir Charles. He is just concluding some business,' Steven said to the familiar and expected face.

'Thank you, Major,' Sir Charles Hadleigh said, 'I know he is a busy man and appreciate him seeing me at this late hour.' He was feeling pleased that Cromwell had agreed to see him, and knew that with just a little patience, he and his fellow concerned MPs and friends would have the signature that would put an end to the outrageous demands of the agitators threatening the natural order. After little more than one minute, Cromwell's voice was heard from the other side of the room.

'Come in, Major!'

Inside the shadowed room, lit at this late hour by candles, Sir Charles Hadleigh walked towards the table where Cromwell sat with Jonathan Litchfield, stopped and bowed at a respectful distance.

'Good evening, Sir Charles, I hope you are well and assume you are here on important business, to be calling at this late hour,' Cromwell said.

'Yes, sir. I believe it is most urgent. I have an arrest warrant for a number of agitators for the crimes of heresy and sedition, as we discussed. We can catch many of them tomorrow morning as we believe most are in London. We also believe some may be planning to flee England after spreading their propaganda. This is our chance to seize them, and to lance the boil on the body of our country,' Sir Charles said.

'Well, I am not sure if it will put an end to all agitators, Sir Charles, but if you have their names and we can arrest some of them, it will be a step in the right direction,' Cromwell said encouragingly.

'Yes. sir,' Hadleigh replied, feeling relieved Cromwell was seeing sense and supporting his efforts, particularly after previous conversations where he felt he was having to persuade the Lord Protector to take action.

'Very good, Sir Charles. Let me have the warrant.'

Sir Charles stepped up to the table, unrolled the

parchment he had held in his left hand, laid it out on the table and took three steps back to allow Cromwell and his aide to examine the document, without his shadow. Cromwell and Jonathan pored over the warrant for a minute, inspecting each name with the respect it deserved.

'Good work, Sir Charles,' Cromwell said quietly, but loud enough for the MP to hear, providing him with further reassurance by adding, 'Let us snare our prey.' With that, Cromwell reached forward for the quill, dipped it into the ink and proceeded to sign the warrant, but there was a problem.

'Ah, no! This quill is broken, Jonathan,' and the warrant had a blotch of ink instead of a signature.

'Oh no!' Sir Charles said, fearing he would not have his signed warrant that night.

'I am sorry, sir,' Litchfield said, 'we have more quills here,' and he turned to the table behind them.

'Very well, here…' Cromwell said and stood up, handing the warrant to his aide, who laid it out on the table a few steps back to the other table at the back of the room. The warrant was signed, tied with a thin red ribbon, and handed back to Sir Charles, who was relieved as it was handed to him by the aide and bowed solemnly.

'Thank you, sir. We will arrest these heretical seditionists tomorrow, and England will be a safer place.'

'Excellent, Sir Charles. You have important work to do tomorrow and I wish you God's speed,' Cromwell replied, wishing to conclude the business, 'and I am tired. Good night, Sir Charles.'

'Yes, sir. Thank you again, and a good night to you, sir.' Hadleigh bowed again, turned and left the room pleased with his night's work. He would enjoy some wine in his private quarters before bed and deliver the warrant to Colonel Harris at first light.

After Hadleigh had closed the door, Cromwell looked at Steven.

'Steven, I think we must take action tonight and early

tomorrow, lest some good people are hurt in Sir Charles Hadleigh's purge.'

'Yes, sir,' Steven replied, and he joined the two men at the large wooden table.

15th June 1654

'They're coming, you must leave now!' Steven said in a firm but hushed voice. John Wiggett and Joanne Aker looked up to see an anguished look on the face of the Major they had come to trust. It was dark, save for a few candles, the last customers having left a while ago, leaving them to perform the daily ritual of tidying the tavern before bed and sleep. Following the warning from Steven three days earlier, they had each prepared a bag, carefully tucked away in the kitchen. John had also gathered the coins he had stored in various places over the years. The nervous anticipation of the previous three nights had resulted in only broken sleep, but they were ready.

'Where to, sir?' John asked.

'Down to the river, John. Follow me and I will explain once we are clear of danger,' Steven replied. He led them out of the tavern, John closing the solid wooden door for the last time. It was a clear sky, which helped their visibility, but the shadows cast by the buildings made the small street leading to Whitehall very dark, so Steven instinctively held Joanne's hand, who realised this was the first time he had physically touched her.

Rather than follow the wider road of Whitehall, which afforded them more light, Steven turned left taking them through small streets and alleys leading gently downhill to the river. If the troop of soldiers sent to arrest them at the Three Tuns was close, it was likely they would approach along the bigger road from Westminster.

Within minutes Steven had them safely down at the riverbank, just a quarter of a mile from Parliament. He paused and whispered, 'Just a moment,' as he looked along the riverbank for the jetty known as Charing Cross Steps where he and Joanne had been in January, but in the dark, Joanne did not recognise it, nor could she recognise the wherryman Steven knew would be waiting. About forty yards away a small light from a lantern cast a glimmer across the water, and he hoped that was their man. 'Follow me, I think this is our boat,' and as they approached, he called, 'Sergeant Moore!' Steven was relieved to hear the reply, 'Yes, Major. This way, but take care on the jetty, it is wet and slippery.'

Holding Joanne's hand, Steven led them along the short wooden jetty towards the lantern held by a man who was formerly Sergeant Paul Moore, who had served with Steven when he was just a captain, but had now returned to his family trade of wherryman. They climbed down into the small boat and Paul cast off using the oars to push them clear of the bank towards the middle of the river.

'I am relieved to see you, Paul,' Steven said.

'As I am to you see you, sir,' Paul replied, adding, 'Where is our destination, sir?'

'St Katherine's Pier, just past the Tower, please, Paul.'

'Right you are, sir. If you could hold this lantern for us, I will have you there soon enough.'

Steven held the light providing some visibility for the oarsman, who leaned into his task. With only the slightest sound as the oars entered the water, Paul moved the boat to midstream, where the current was strongest and to their benefit. It also made it less likely that they might collide with a moored vessel in the darkness. Occasionally, they would pass other faint lights low on the banks either side, denoting other wherrymen waiting for night-time customers, and above them some brighter lights from houses and churches. Apart from those, the city was shrouded in darkness and quiet, creating an eerie atmosphere that made Joanne feel uncomfortable and she huddled close to her uncle for security at the back of the small boat. John also felt nervous and found himself whispering.

'Sir, where are we bound?'

Steven was sat at the front of the boat holding the lantern, looking out for any potential hazards. 'It is safe to speak, John, I do not think we can be overheard here at this hour. And do not fear, I trust Sergeant Paul Moore with my life,' he said reassuringly. 'As I said three days ago, it is no longer safe for you to remain in this land, so you are bound for the Americas. There is a ship waiting at St Katherine's Pier, which will take you to a safer place, where dissent is tolerated.'

John felt relieved to know they were bound for a safe place, as well as a little sad that they were leaving his home and livelihood at the Three Tuns. But he was ready for a change. Joanne did not feel regret at leaving behind her life in a London tavern. It had provided her with home and food, but she was tired of the lustful advances of men emboldened after two cups of ale. However, she did feel sadness that she would never again see the young officer she had come to admire, who sat holding the lantern at the front of the wherry.

'Very good, sir. I hear there are great opportunities in the Americas,' John said.

'I hope you brought everything you need for the voyage, and I have some money to help you establish yourselves in a new land,' Steven replied. He and Cromwell felt some guilt for the situation that led to these honest people having to flee, so £30 in silver coins was secure with Steven to be handed to John shortly before they set sail.

'That's very kind of you, sir,' John replied, not knowing how much they might be given, just grateful to be escaping Parliament's so-called justice.

After twenty-five minutes, helped by a kindly current, they had journeyed the distance of almost two miles along the river, and they knew they were getting closer to St Katherine's Pier as they passed under London Bridge. Looking up they could see the houses and shops, buildings lit by lanterns inside and outside, providing some safety for pedestrians crossing at night. Five minutes later more lights, this time high above the level of the river, spaced at equal distances, told them they were passing the Tower, and there just past the east wall of the Tower was a long pier protruding into the river.

'Here we are, sirs, and miss. St Katherine's Pier,' the wherryman said as he smoothly turned the boat to the left by reversing the stroke of his left-hand oar. 'It looks as though you were expected, Major,' he added as he spotted a man holding a lantern waiting on the jetty beside the great wooden structure that was the pier.

The man's lantern revealed a familiar face to Steven. 'Good evening, Sergeant Barthrop,' he called, as the wherry came to a gentle halt against the jetty just as Paul Moore pulled in the oars.

'Hello, sir, I would say good evening but I think I heard a bell announce midnight a while ago, so good morning might be more accurate,' Sergeant Barthrop replied with a smile, adding, 'It is good to see you here safely.' He helped John and Joanne up the four steps onto the jetty as Steven thanked wherryman Paul.

'Thank you, Sergeant,' Steven said, shaking his hand and then using his left hand to place a silver coin in his palm.

Without looking at the coin, Paul Moore said, 'thank you kindly, sir, it has been my pleasure, and God's speed to you all,' and with that he used the oars to push his little boat clear of the jetty and rowed back towards midstream, the light of his lantern fading as he headed upstream towards Westminster.

From the little jetty a step ladder had to be climbed to the pier more than ten feet above them. Sergeant Barthrop took Joanne's bag and placed his left arm through the straps so it hung over his back, then holding the lantern in one hand led them up the ladder.

'Take care, miss,' he said, 'hold the ladder with both hands and you should not end up in the Thames.'

'Thank you, Sergeant,' Joanne replied with a nervous smile.

Having reached St Katherine's Pier from one side in total darkness except for the wherryman's lantern, they were not prepared for the sight they encountered once they were up onto the pier, where in the darkness they could see the shape of a large ship moored alongside the pier.

'Here she is, sir, *The Republic*, let's get you all aboard,' said the sergeant and he led them to the other side of the pier to where a gangplank connected the two great wooden structures, pier and ship.

'Thank you, Sergeant,' Steven replied, and they were soon below deck, where they were shown to their cabins.

'Try to get some sleep and hopefully we will sail in the morning,' Steven said, and once inside their cabins each of them settled into their bunks in an attempt to do as the Major advised.

John and Joanne awoke in the morning, having drifted in and out of sleep. Joanne felt some sadness thinking, 'That's it, he's gone. We will set sail and I will never see Major Flain again. Perhaps it was unrealistic for me to think otherwise, me a barmaid, him an officer.' She sighed and joined her uncle on deck.

In the light of day John and Joanne could fully appreciate the size and majesty of the vessel they had boarded in the dark six hours earlier. Stepping onto the main deck they felt dwarfed by three great masts reaching up to the sky, and they were soon joined by thirty or so other passengers, who having arrived the previous evening as the sun was setting, could also now see *The Republic* properly. None of the sails were lowered so the ship seemed to consist solely of great masts, cross masts and rigging. Standing just yards from the former residents of the Three Tuns were Jeremy, Michael and their families, who were unknown to them but were on the ship for the same purpose. However, Joanne suddenly became aware of the two men from Barnet as she overheard Michael say to Jeremy, 'There's Major Flain.' Joanne turned to look at Michael who was facing the raised poop deck at the rear of the ship, to where she immediately looked. She felt a sense of relief as she saw Steven standing alongside another distinguished looking man in a different kind of uniform, who she guessed must be the captain of the ship, and was confirmed by him pointing and issuing orders to a variety of men all about them. As she stared at him, Steven was looking at the crowd gathered on the main deck and he spotted her, standing just twenty yards away next to her uncle. He instinctively raised his hand as if to wave but hesitated and a wide smile appeared on his face. 'He's still here,' she thought, as she raised her hand and smiled back.

Steven had stood with Captain Philip Ames surveying the scene before them, in which the crew was busy preparing *The Republic* for setting sail, whilst in the middle of the main deck the passengers had gathered as requested to see who be might be missing, or yet to arrive. Sergeant Barthrop joined them on the poop deck.

'Good morning, Sergeant. Thank you for your efforts to get us safely to this point in our venture,' Steven said.

'Thank you, sir. All seems to have gone smoothly so far,' Barthrop replied.

'Are all of the passengers present, Major? I would like to set sail down to the estuary and get clear of London as soon as there is a kind wind. Once we're out into open water we can take our time,' Captain Ames said, conscious of the danger of being intercepted whilst moored to the pier. Steven had been trying to count the numbers on deck, but found it difficult as the gathered passengers were continually moving about.

'I wish we could call them into line, Captain. A company of soldiers would be easier. What do you say, Sergeant?' Steven said, seeking assistance from Andrew Barthrop.

'I've counted thirty-two adults, sir. Which means we are two bodies light, and I think they are the two men who were staying at the Swan Inn last night,' Barthrop replied.

'David Davies and Gavin Evans,' Steven said, asking, 'Did you tell them to be here at sunrise, Sergeant?'

'Yes, sir, I told them of the arrangements last night.'

Twenty minutes earlier, Gavin Evans woke in the room he had shared with David Davies upstairs in the Swan Inn. His head was aching from at least three cups of ale too many the previous night. Despite the importance of being punctual the next day, he and his countryman could not resist having their fill as it might be the last time in a tavern for many weeks. But any fog in his head was cleared as he heard nearby church bells ring six times.

'Dear God!' he exclaimed and jumped to his feet. 'David, we are late and must make haste.'

'What time is it, Gavin?'

'Six bells just rang, so the ship will sail once there is sufficient wind,' Gavin replied.

The two men rose from their beds, dressed and began to gather their possessions, which would be contained in one large bag each, but before they could complete the task, they heard loud banging below.

'Someone is at the door!' David said, and went to the small window that looked out across the front courtyard, slightly moving the dirty curtain. 'They're here, Gavin, a troop of guards! Leave the rest, we must flee, or face arrest.'

Taking their bags with the possessions they had managed to gather, David led Gavin out of their small room at the front of the inn, stepping quietly across the corridor to rooms facing the back yard. One of the doors was ajar, allowing them to see the room was empty and there was a window, through which a man might climb. Without delay David opened the window to see that it was only about twelve feet to the ground of the back yard. He climbed through the tight space and lowered himself as far as he could before releasing his grip on the window frame and falling the seven or eight feet to the ground. The sound was no more than a soft thud as he landed on the small untidy vegetable garden. Gavin tossed the two bags to David and within seconds had repeated the manoeuvre. There was no need for discussion, they had to get around the building to the alley leading out to Holborn Bridge, without being seen by the troop of guards at the front of the building. Creeping around the side of the inn they listened carefully to hear someone announce, 'We have a warrant for the arrest of men charged with heresy and sedition, search every…' and then the voice died away, boots on gravel the only sound as the troop entered the Swan. David peeked around the corner to see two guards left at the door, but they were looking straight ahead, so with the nod of his head he gestured for Gavin to follow him as he kept close to the neighbouring wall and they made their escape. One of the guards heard a rustle but when he looked the narrow alley provided enough shadow for the two men to be unidentifiable. 'Bloody vagabonds and street urchins,' the guard said to his fellow sentry.

Hugging the wall of the alleyway, David and Gavin crept away from the Swan, knowing one way or another they would probably never set foot inside again. The alley was in such shade that David almost stumbled over a small boy crouched down against the wall, where he may have slept that night. 'Sorry, lad,' David whispered as he stepped over the small creature dressed in rags and with no footwear. David paused, reached into his pocket and gave the boy a penny.

'Not now, David, we must make haste,' Gavin whispered, and his countryman continued along the darkened alleyway.

Out of the alley and onto Holborn Bridge, they could smell the contents of the River Fleet flowing just to their right, but they turned left away from the foul stench which disappeared as they broke into a trot. Coming to a junction, they paused and could safely speak for the first time since they left their room at the Swan.

'That troop looked to number about twenty, if they have an inkling of where we are heading, they will soon be behind us. Two of us can make quicker progress than their number, so we should not tarry,' David said.

'Aye, lead the way, David, without handing out any more alms to the poor,' Gavin replied.

Both men, raised in the Welsh hills, had always been fit and enjoyed success in army foot races for light relief and sport within their regiment, when there was no combat. So, when

David broke into a run along Snow Hill towards Newgate, Gavin was able to follow close behind.

David was correct in his assessment and as they got to where Snow Hill turned gently left and became Newgate, the troop of twenty emerged from the darkness of the alley onto Holborn Bridge, having thoroughly searched every room at the Swan Inn for persons and possible evidence of agitators. Unfortunately, their leader, Captain Popejoy, had an idea of where they should go next to apprehend them.

'Follow me, men. They may be looking to flee the country, so we will look for them at the docks,' said the young Captain, and he led the troop at a brisk march in the direction taken by their prey.

From the Swan Inn to St Katherine's Pier was a distance of about two miles, which the two Welshmen could cover in no more than eleven minutes in a foot race wearing light shoes. But in full dress, wearing boots and carrying a bag, they should be able to reach their destination in about fifteen minutes, if they did not tarry. David knew the route, so they proceeded without pausing along Newgate Street, passing the great church of St Paul's on their right, then down Cheapside, Poultry Street, Lombard Street and Fenchurch Street. Halfway along Fenchurch Street they turned right on Mince Street and then left on Tower Street. In the pleasant summer morning both men had started to perspire heavily, but aside from breathing more deeply they were able to press on until they emerged from Tower Street at the open space around the moat and outer wall of the Tower itself. Stopping to catch their breath, David pointed left towards the rising terrain of Tower Hill, where so many men and women had been executed.

'We can follow the moat around the Tower to St Katherine's Pier, where I hope the ship is still waiting,' David said.

'Good, let's not tarry,' Gavin replied, and so the two men resumed their foot race, the prize being their freedom.

Steven, Captain Ames and Sergeant Barthrop stood on

the poop deck discussing whether to wait for the two missing passengers if and when the wind provided an opportunity to sail.

'No, we can't wait. To do so endangers the liberty of many of these people in front of us,' Steven said, his eyes drawn to Joanne and her uncle. The thought of the young woman being hauled before a jury facing charges of heresy and sedition was unbearable.

'Very good, sir,' Captain Ames said, relieved that the voyage would not be jeopardised by two late-comers, and that he might not be charged with assisting fugitives. 'We set sail as soon as possible!' he added, and as he did so two men appeared at the end of the pier, running and carrying bags.

'Looks like you might have a full complement after all, sir,' Sergeant Barthrop said.

The heavily perspiring pair of Welshmen only stopped running once they had arrived at the gangplank connecting *The Republic* to the pier, walking slowly and carefully the last three yards onto the ship.

'Room for two more, sir?' David Davies said with a smile.

'Aye, but you've cut it fine, gentlemen,' Captain Ames called out from the poop deck.

Sergeant Barthrop muttered something under his breath, unimpressed with their punctuality, whispering to Steven, 'Well, my duty has been performed, sir, so I will leave you to get underway. But I will wait until you leave before reporting back to the Lord Protector that the operation was successful.'

Steven leaned his head towards Barthrop, saying, 'We are all indebted to you, Sergeant. You have my heartfelt thanks, which I ask you to please pass on to the Lord Protector.'

'Yes, sir. I will pass those words to the Lord Protector, and it has been a pleasure to work with you.' With those last words, Sergeant Barthrop climbed down the steps from the poop deck to the main deck, walked past the two late arrivals, affording them a polite nod, made his way to the gangplank and onto the pier. The gathering of dissenters fleeing England in search of freedom of conscience, escaping possible trial, prison and worse, were ignorant of the part played by the brave Sergeant in their drama, as he modestly passed through their ranks.

With everyone aboard Captain Ames waited for a breeze that could be employed to take them down the Thames, out of the estuary and into the North Sea, before turning south and west to enter the Channel and finally the Atlantic. As he did so, Sergeant Barthrop stayed on the pier waiting for them to safely depart, which he could then report to Cromwell. As the minutes passed both he and Captain Ames became nervous, it being their misfortune that particular morning was calm, with little or no wind, the Thames resembling a mill pond. On the main deck the passengers did not share their nervousness, instead choosing their vantage points from which to look at London for the last time once the ship was moving. All of the crew was ready as well, standing in teams at the base of the three masts, and at various rigging points around the ship.

However, it was all to be in vain as onto the pier marched the troop of twenty soldiers, led by Captain Popejoy. They arrived twenty minutes after David and Gavin, having marched through several docks looking for the fugitives, but now they were on the pier that would end their search. The young Captain sensed they might be closing in on their prey as he saw a ship populated by civilians waiting to depart. 'Where are they going?' he wondered, as he approached the gangplank.

Steven saw the troop approach only at the last moment as standing on the poop deck he and Captain Ames were facing forward towards midstream. He felt a chill through his spine and his throat became dry seeing a captain and twenty soldiers file across the wooden board onto *The Republic*. Sergeant Barthrop had seen them a minute earlier when he turned from looking at the river, but it was too late to raise an alarm and he tried to think of something he could do.

'I have here a warrant for the arrest of men and women who are charged with the crimes of heresy and sedition. Who is the master of this vessel? And I require a full list of the crew and passengers. This is by order of Parliament,' Captain Popejoy announced loudly so everyone could hear, adding, 'No one is to leave the ship!' As he spoke his troop fanned into a line along the side of the deck with the pier to their backs.

Steven and Captain Ames stepped down from the poop deck to speak to the young Captain. Steven was his senior officer, but he knew that would not be an effective weapon if the warrant has been signed by someone more senior than himself.

'What warrant do you speak of, Captain?' Steven asked, trying to delay proceedings while he thought of a possible escape, but he was not optimistic. 'Dear God, the game is up,' he thought, immediately fearing for Joanne.

'Sir, I have here a warrant for the arrest of men and women listed, some of whom I believe aboard a ship bound for the Americas,' Captain Popejoy replied, producing a parchment from his tunic. 'Captain,' he said turning to Ames, 'you must show me a list of all your crew and passengers, immediately, or face the full force of the law.' The young officer felt emboldened by the position he had assumed in the unfolding drama, as not a sound was heard on the deck and everyone's eyes were fixed on him.

'Who is this warrant signed by?' Steven asked, again trying to delay the inevitable. 'Perhaps the warrant can be questioned?' he thought.

A grin appeared on the face of Captain Popejoy, which had hitherto been stern, as he was hoping such an objection might be made. 'The signature befits the seriousness of the charges, Major. It is signed by no less than the Lord Protector himself!' he said, again nice and loud so everyone could hear. Steven felt as though he had been punched in the stomach, as the situation seemed to be hopeless.

'Captain, the list of crew and passengers, if you please,' Popejoy asked, which left Captain Ames with no choice but to comply.

'Lieutenant Atwood, would you go to my cabin and bring the ship's register,' Ames said to a young naval officer standing to his right, who promptly turned and disappeared through the door leading to the area below the poop deck. A minute later he returned with a thick leather-bound book and handed it to Captain Ames. The book was laid down on a deck cupboard used to store rigging and Ames opened the book, turning to the latest page with writing, dated 15th June 1654, with the title *Providence, Americas Colonies.*

'Here you are, Captain,' Ames said to the army officer.

As everyone watched, Captain Popejoy unfolded the parchment and laid it out next to the ship's register, allowing him to check the two lists to find the names that appeared in both. With a piece of chalk, he could match those names on his list with those in the ship's register. After some minutes, which felt like an hour to everyone watching, he looked up.

'Seven, sir!' he said speaking to Steven. There are seven people on this warrant signed by the Lord Protector, who are also on this ship!' he announced. 'This ship is now impounded by Parliament, and no person shall leave it until the seven persons are found or accounted for. Captain Ames, every member of the crew and every passenger will have to be identified against the register,' Popejoy added.

'Yes, Captain,' Ames replied with a sigh, realising he had no choice but to comply. He had a crew of 120, who could overpower twenty soldiers, but at what cost. There could be bloodshed and his defiance of the arrest warrant would probably mean he could never return to England. Everyone, the crew and the passengers were on the main deck listening, so they were all aware of what was happening.

'Lieutenant Atwood,' Captain Ames said, 'get the crew to fall in to line, and organise the passengers to do the same.' He thought a formal line-up might provide a bit more time, during which something might happen to change the inevitable outcome. But any delay was undermined by a voice from the passengers.

'That won't be necessary, Captain. You can just call out the seven names, and I think I am one of them. David Davies, sir.' The unmistakeable welsh lilt in the resigned voice of David Davies was followed by him stepping forward.

'And Gavin Evans is also probably one of the seven, sir,' another welsh voice said, and he stepped forward to stand alongside his friend.

After a pause, both Jeremy Odlin and Michael Martin stepped forward stating their names. Then there was quiet, as the last three names were persons who were uncertain about being on the warrant list. Captain Popejoy looked down at his list to the three remaining names marked with chalk, then up at the passengers.

'The last three are...' he paused, 'Harry Clarke, John Wiggett, and Joanne Aker.' There was a gasp with the announcement of the last name and Steven saw Joanne in the crowd almost collapse, prevented from doing so by the support of her uncle. Steven felt a stomach-churning wrench and he wanted to go to her, but knew he had to remain still, lest he incriminate himself. He began to feel a dreadful guilt that he had brought this honest man and his niece to this end. If he had not taken Cromwell to their inn six months earlier, they would not have been drawn into this web. If he had not felt such a strong attraction for Joanne, he would not have pursued their involvement. Now they faced arrest and possibly worse. Should he confess his part in the plot to save them? Or would he just be joining them in court?

'Come, Joanne, all will be well,' John said to the niece who had become a daughter. He was speaking from hope, rather than confidence, but had to offer her something as tears streamed down her cheeks. The crew watched as the two of them moved forward to stand alongside the four men.

'That leaves just Harry Clarke...' Popejoy said.

'That's me, sir,' a voice replied and a young man, no more than a boy, stepped forward.

There was a murmur amongst the crowd on hearing the last two names, particularly some members of the crew, as they could understand men being named for heresy and sedition. Seamen were familiar with the stories of former soldiers joining organisations calling for reform. Such men knew what they were doing, but the crew did not think young women and boys were likely to be guilty of such crimes. The disquiet was tangible, and some members of the crew moved forward meaningfully towards the officers and the troop of soldiers, the threat of resistance clear for all to see. Captain Popejoy looked at the crew as a good number of them, more than he would want to fight, edged towards him. His troop of men instinctively drew their swords, combat seeming unavoidable, but it was halted by Steven stepping forward, his arms raised. However, it wasn't his voice that halted the crew from attacking the soldiers.

'Stand down, you men!' bellowed someone from behind the soldiers, someone standing on the pier. His voice was deep and powerful, a voice used to being projected across a hall or a field.

Make way, you men!' Called another loud voice, 'We're coming aboard!' The second of the voices was Sergeant Barthrop, who was first across the gangplank holding his own sword and made sure a space was cleared for those who followed. Behind him walked a man familiar to Steven, and recognised by Captain Popejoy, John and Joanne, as well as a few of the soldiers, but not by the other 150 or so persons stood on the main deck.

Oliver Cromwell strode across the gangplank with a purpose that belied his fifty-five years of age, followed by his two personal guards. A further twelve dragoons who had accompanied him on horseback at great haste through the streets of London from Westminster, remained on the pier, as Cromwell did not think they would be required.

'Stand down, I said,' he bellowed again at the crew and soldiers who were still too close and clearly still nervous. This drew their attention and suddenly a whisper amongst several of the soldiers spread, 'The Lord Protector, lower your weapons,' and almost immediately the crew also realised to whom they were listening. Taking two or three steps back the crew resumed their passive stance, allowing space for Cromwell and his guard of three to walk between them and the troop of soldiers to where Popejoy, Ames and Flain were stood. He saw John and Joanne but desisted from revealing any knowledge of them, and hoped they would do the same.

'Captain Popejoy, are you in charge of this operation?' Cromwell asked, knowing the answer, but affording the young captain a chance to explain himself.

'Yes, sir,' Popejoy replied nervously, surprised that the Lord Protector should know his name, but still confident he was doing his rightful duty. 'I have a warrant from Parliament, signed by yourself, to arrest agitators guilty of heresy and sedition, sir.'

'Have you indeed, Captain? Heresy and sedition, you say. They are serious crimes, Captain. I came here to see off a ship taking good English men and women to the New World to spread the Word of God. It is quite a coincidence that I should find you here arresting some of them,' Cromwell said.

'Yes, sir,' Popejoy replied, beginning to wonder if something was amiss.

'Well, I thank you for your rigour and duty, Captain, as we do not want fugitives guilty of serious crimes fleeing to the Americas. So, I bid you continue with apprehending the suspects.'

'Yes, sir,' Popejoy said with some relief, and was about to order the seven to be taken ashore.

'Before you do, Captain, may I see the warrant you claim I signed? I sign many documents each day, but do not recall such a warrant.'

'Of course, sir, I have it here,' and the young captain

picked up the parchment from the cupboard, where it lay with the ship's register, and respectfully handed it to his master. There was a pause and silence as Cromwell read the document.

'By my word, from where did you get this warrant, Captain?' Cromwell asked as he looked up from the parchment, staring with a look of anger at the young officer.

'Sir?' Popejoy asked, confused.

'From where, or whom, did you get this warrant, Captain Popejoy?' Cromwell asked with a cold accusatory tone.

'Sir, I, I was given it by Colonel Harris, sir, and told to carry out the arrest,' Popejoy said, his collar feeling tight and uncomfortable. But he could not move to loosen the irritation.

'Captain Popejoy, it is most fortunate for you that I came to see off this ship, because you appear to have been caught up in something very sinister. This is a calumny, a fraud, an injustice, sir.' Cromwell's voice was raised to convey his ire and the seriousness of the situation.

'Sir? Have I done something wrong?' the young officer asked, his heart pounding and fearful for his position.

'Captain, I do not believe you have deliberately done anything wrong, but you have been used by men more senior as a pawn. Look, Captain,' Cromwell said, pointing at the bottom of the parchment, but Popejoy could see nothing irregular.

'Sir?' he asked, relieved he was not himself accused or guilty of wrongdoing, but confused at what was faulty with the warrant.

'Forgive me, Captain,' Cromwell said ameliorating his tone, 'You are not to be expected to be familiar with my signature, but your senior officers and the politicians who employed you should be. But what you have missed, for which I will discipline you, is there is no Seal of State, Captain. Look!' Cromwell held up the warrant for the young officer to see, as well as anyone else close enough. Sure enough, there was no wax seal, which the Head of State and Government would use to confirm authenticity. 'Sergeant Barthrop, would you be so kind to confirm this is not my signature and whether my seal has been applied to this warrant?'

Andrew Barthrop stepped forward and examined the document. 'I have never seen that signature before, sir, and I have seen your signature many times, having the privilege of serving you in the offices of Westminster, sir,' the Sergeant said loud and clear.

'And the seal, Sergeant?'

'There is no seal, sir. Anyone can see that,' Barthrop replied.

The mood amongst the crew and the passengers was transformed, not least for the seven stood in a line in front of the officers. David Davies could not suppress a smile and put his arm around the shoulder of his friend. Joanne's tears were wiped away saying, 'Thank you, sir.'

Cromwell looked over at Joanne and allowed himself a modest smile at the young woman he had come to respect. 'It is my duty to stop any injustice carried out against the people, miss. I am sorry for any ordeal you have suffered.' He wished he could have more time to listen to Joanne and her uncle, but he knew he had to see the theatrics through to the end and they would be the last words he would ever speak to her. Turning to Captain Popejoy, he decided the affair on *The Republic* should be concluded and the ship should be allowed to get underway. 'Well, Captain Popejoy, I suggest you accompany me back to Westminster, but I see you are on foot, whereas I and my guard have horses.'

'Yes, sir. What would you have me do, sir?' the relieved Captain asked.

'Captain Popejoy, I have been impressed with your rigour, albeit with some error regarding the missing seal. With guidance I am sure you can improve to become a valuable member of my personal guard. And I need some assistance today in arresting the perpetrators of this injustice.'

'Yes, sir,' Popejoy replied, asking 'Shall my troop and I make our way back to Westminster now, sir?'

'Yes, Captain Popejoy, I think you should make haste, lest the foxes we hunt take flight. I would like to wish the Captain of *The Republic*, its crew and passengers a safe passage, then my guard and I will shortly be along behind you. Report to my office quarters at the Palace of Westminster.'

'Yes, sir, Captain Popejoy replied, and with some relief he led his troop across the gangplank onto the pier, from where they made their way back to Westminster at a brisk march.

Cromwell turned to Captain Ames, asking him quietly, 'I will tarry a while longer to wish you, your crew and the passengers a safe voyage, Captain. But before I do, I see you have another senior army officer here on your ship. May I ask you to indulge me, by allowing me to speak to him privately.'

'Of course, sir. Would you like to use my cabin?' Ames replied.

'Actually, I think your poop deck will suffice, so anyone can see us, making suspicion less likely.'

'Of course, sir.'

'Major! Would you follow me,' Cromwell said loudly, and climbed the steps to the empty poop deck, followed by Steven, adopting a suitably worried look, which belied the immense relief he felt inside.

Up on the raised poop deck, Cromwell walked five steps towards the rear of the ship, so they were visible to everyone but too far to be heard. 'I will be brief, Steven, lest we raise suspicion. This is where our paths diverge, you bound for the New World, me returning to Parliament. I would like to shake your hand, perhaps even hug you, such is my gratitude for your service and the respect I have come to feel, but our audience precludes such gestures. So, without a smile I wish you good health and prosperity.'

'Thank you, sir. I too am unable to express my respect and gratitude for everything you have given me,' Steven said with a heavy heart realising this would be the last time they spoke.

'Oh, and one other thing, Steven.'

'Yes, sir?'

'Do the right thing regarding that young woman,' and as he spoke Cromwell glanced over to where Joanne stood, to see her smile and eyes fixed on him and Steven, adding, 'God bless you both.' With those words Cromwell walked over to the steps down to the main deck and descended to where Captain Ames stood, with whom he walked amongst the crew and passengers.

Steven stood and surveyed the scene piecing together what had happened. His respect for the man he had said goodbye to, increased as it sank in what he had done. Steven was there, stood by the door in the Lord Protector's office the previous evening. He saw the arrest warrant produced by Sir Charles Hadleigh, who had to wait as there was a problem with the quill used for the signature. Cromwell had complained to his aide and they took the parchment to the back of the room to another table and new quills. They had their backs to Steven and Sir Charles as they leaned over the table to sign the warrant. Both Cromwell and his aide, Jonathan Litchfield, held a quill but facing their backs, it was not clear to Steven and Sir Charles what they were doing. The sound of quill on parchment could be heard, the Seal of State was raised and brought down with care and purpose, but it was not clear onto what it fell. Cromwell, showing impatience with the whole procedure, held up the warrant for Sir Charles to see, before the document was rolled and tied with a ribbon by Litchfield, who handed it to Hadleigh. Cromwell had taken a risk that Sir Charles Hadleigh would not closely examine the warrant and was proved right, knowing the MP was in a hurry to make the arrests before the agitators fled. So it was that the warrant with Cromwell's signature, forged by a trusted aide and without his seal, was handed to Sir Charles Hadleigh, who passed it to Colonel Harris, who gave it to Captain Popejoy.

As Steven made sense of it all in his mind, he looked down to see Cromwell had finished his well-wishing with the men and women who would be sailing across the Atlantic on

The Republic, and with one last glance up to the poop deck he raised his hand. Steven replied with a salute.

Cromwell walked across the gangplank, followed by Sergeant Barthrop and two personal guards, and made their way to their horses at the end of the pier, where they joined the troop of dragoons. As Cromwell and his men climbed onto their horses, there was a change in the atmosphere, which went unnoticed by the passengers, but not by the crew.

'Lieutenant Atwood!' Captain Ames bellowed as he climbed the steps to his rightful place on the poop deck. 'Is that a favourable wind, Lieutenant Atwood?'

From the main deck came the reply, 'Aye, sir. I believe it is,' the young officer replied and walked up the steps to join his master.

'Then let's get all hands on deck, Lieutenant,' the captain said.

'They are already on deck, Captain,' the Lieutenant said with a cheeky smile, which was met with, 'So they are. Then let's set sail,' by Captain Ames with a smile of his own.

The great wooden leviathan became a machine as mooring ropes were untied and rigging was pulled tight. A small army of men climbed the three masts to unfurl the sails and *The Republic* moved gently away from St Katherine's Pier.

Feeling as though he was in the way on the poop deck, Steven took his leave from Captain Ames, went down to the main deck and fixed his eyes on Joanne, who was stood to the side, trying to keep out of the way of the crew going about their business oblivious of the passengers. She looked up to see Steven as he approached, unable to suppress her joy at seeing him, but confused that he was still on the ship.

'Major Flain, shouldn't you be on land by now? We are leaving. Or are you sailing with us until we are clear of London?'

'I brought my bag, Joanne,' Steven replied holding up his own bag of possessions.

'Sir?' was all Joanne could say, hopeful but still

uncertain.

'I decided it was time to leave England, and I was wondering if you and your uncle would allow me to accompany you?' he replied with a smile.

'Sir, I think we would like that,' was all Joanne could say with a smile as wide as her face, and she leaned forward kissing him on the cheek.

'Then I think, henceforth, you should call me Steven,' he said, wrapping his arms around her in a warm embrace.